Maid For a Sheikh

Kate Goldman

Maid For a Sheikh

Published by Kate Goldman

Copyright © 2019 by Kate Goldman

ISBN 978-1-07044-040-8

First printing, 2019

www.KateGoldmanBooks.com

PRINTED IN THE UNITED STATES OF AMERICA

Dedication

I want to dedicate this book to my beloved husband, who makes every day in my life worthwhile. Thank you for believing in me when nobody else does, giving me encouragement when I need it the most, and loving me simply for being myself.

Table of Contents

Chapter 1

Jane

Jane tucked the price tag into her skirt as she nervously walked up the stone path leading to the massive house. She had bought her skirt for her interview, and she was intending to return it afterwards. She needed to get that job by all means. She needed the money.

Jane noticed how nice the neatly cut grass was. The green stretched for miles. Beautiful flowers lined the path leading to the three-story house. She had never been on that side of Boston; the elite side for the wealthy. Jane walked up the concrete steps and approached the large wooden door. She pressed the doorbell.

The door swung open and a woman dressed in white appeared. "Good afternoon," she said with a smile.

"Good afternoon. My name is Jane and I am here for an interview," said Jane. She tucked a stray tendril of hair behind her ear. She had her hair tied up into a ponytail but she always had a stubborn lock or two that got left out.

"Please follow me," the woman said to Jane.

Jane followed her into the house. She gaped at the place as she followed quietly. The totally clean floors were made of white marble. They walked into a large room with high ceilings and white and gold furniture. A woman was sitting on one of two sofas. She wore an expensive-looking peach dress. She had her hair pinned into a low bun. She looked quite elegant. Jane wondered if she was the wife.

"Miss Tadros, Jane is here," the woman in white said to the elegant woman on the sofa. The woman looked up.

"Miss Hart, please have a seat," she said to Jane.

"Thank you." Jane sat down on the sofa opposite her. Miss Tadros had some paperwork and a phone on her lap.

"I am just working on something for the sheikh," she said as she put the paper on the glass table in front of her.

"Sheikh." The word echoed in Jane's head. Was she interviewing to work for a sheikh? It made sense to her now. On the job post, it had stated that the position was paying $3,000 a month for part-time work. That was quite high for just a maid.

"I am Mariam, the sheikh's assistant," said Miss Tadros.

"Nice to meet you," Jane replied. It was a good thing Mariam had introduced herself because Jane was curious as to who she was.

"I will interview you first, and if you are successful, then you will meet the sheikh. He will make the final decision."

"Sounds fair."

"Right, let us begin." Mariam crossed her right leg over her left knee. Jane felt a little nervous. Mariam had such a cold presence. She hadn't smiled at Jane when she arrived, nor did she shake her hand.

"You are aware that this position requires a cleaner and a cook?" said Mariam.

"Yes," Jane replied.

"Do you have any experience cooking and cleaning?"

No, Jane wanted to say. However, she had learned in the past that experience was always valuable, so she had to think of something fast.

"I do not have professional experience. However, I always cook at home, church cookouts and I've cooked at a few weddings," said Jane. That was a stretch. She had only helped once at her cousin's wedding and she had cooked at two church cookouts.

"What about cleaning?" Mariam asked.

"I was a part-time janitor during my first year of college." At least this was completely true.

"The sheikh is a very particular man. He wants someone that will do the job right and remember everything that he wants done and how to get it done."

"I understand. I am confident that I will learn his needs fast."

"When setting the table, where do you place the salad fork?"

Salad fork? Jane did not even know what a salad fork looked like. She kept her poker face. She did not want to show that she was nervous.

"On the right side of the plate," Jane answered confidently, even though she knew that she was probably wrong. Mariam raised her eyebrows a little.

"Where do you place the water glass?"

"Next to the knife."

"What about the napkins?"

"They are placed underneath the forks." Jane had gone into the interview thinking that she would be asked about recipes or how reliable she was and what kind of skills she was going to bring to the position. She had not anticipated questions about cutlery positioning.

Mariam asked Jane more questions about soups, clearing the table, and Arabic meals. The more questions she asked Jane, the more Jane lost her confidence.

"I ask about small details because Sheikh Asaad is detail-oriented. If you make a tiny error, he will notice," said Mariam as she rose to her feet. Jane also rose to her feet.

"I understand," Jane replied.

"I will be in touch." Mariam's voice gave nothing away. Jane knew that she had botched the interview. She forced a smile and nodded. Jane turned on her heel and left the room. She felt so awkward and disappointed. The position paid well and she needed that money. If she was going to have a shot at completing her master's, she was going to need a well-paying job. Her father's company had filed for bankruptcy, so her parents couldn't pay for her master's.

Jane left Sheikh Asaad's residence and headed back home. She just wanted to get back to job hunting. She had no hopes of hearing back from Mariam.

"How was the interview?" Regina called to Jane as she walked into the house. Regina was Jane's best friend and housemate.

"Terrible," Jane replied as she kicked her shoes off. She headed to the kitchen where Regina was.

"Why?"

Jane opened the fridge and pulled out a can of soda. "I knew nothing. The woman asked me about salad forks and dessert forks." Jane opened her soda and took a sip. Regina laughed.

"I didn't even know a salad fork existed," Regina replied.

"You and I both."

"You might still get the job."

"I doubt it." Jane headed out of the kitchen and to her bedroom. She flipped her laptop open and started looking for jobs. She had completely given up on hearing back from Mariam.

To Jane's surprise, Mariam did call two days later. She asked her to come in for a second interview with the sheikh on that very afternoon. She picked out a blue high-waisted skirt that matched the color of her eyes. Jane topped it off with a loose white blouse and then slipped into a pair of black pointy-toe pumps and rushed out of the house.

She arrived at Sheikh Asaad's residence twenty minutes later. The same woman in white opened the door for her. Jane realized that she was a maid. The maid led her down a different route. The hallways were wide and clean. Beautiful paintings hung on the walls. Jane wanted to admire them but she had an interview to attend. It shocked her that she had gotten it but she was determined to make a good impression on the sheikh.

The maid knocked on the door before she entered. "Miss Hart has arrived," she announced.

"Let her in," a voice replied. Jane could only assume that it was the sheikh's voice.

Jane confidently walked into the room. The sheikh was leaning against his white desk. He had an impressive physique. He was tall and had a muscular build. He wore a crisp white shirt and a pair of khaki trousers. His curly jet-black hair cut was short on the back and sides and complemented his almond-colored skin. He had an attractive three-day stubble that accentuated his strong jawline. He had a straight nose, not too small and not too big. He had dark eyes that immediately made Jane nervous.

She almost lost her footing as she walked towards him and stumbled forward a little. Jane immediately wanted the ground to just open up and swallow her. She felt so embarrassed. She quickly regained her composure.

"Jane Hart," she said to Sheikh Asaad as she approached him. She extended her hand for a handshake.

"Sheikh Asaad." He placed his palm into hers firmly. "Are you alright?" he asked.

"I am fine." Jane knew that he was being polite but she wanted to pretend as if nothing happened. She was too embarrassed to even keep eye contact.

"Have a seat." He pointed at the tufted chair at the desk.

"Thank you," Jane said as she sat down. Sheikh Asaad sat at the chair opposite her.

"To get straight to the point, I am looking for someone competent to work for me part-time," he said. His voice was husky and commanding. Sheikh Asaad leaned back in his chair with his gaze fixed on Jane. "Do you know much about Arabic food?" he asked her.

"Yes, I do. I can cook several dishes and I am willing to learn those that I do not know," she replied. Surely that was the correct answer. However, Sheikh Asaad's facial expression remained blank.

"Can you make hummus from scratch?"

"Yes, I can." She wondered if that was a serious question. She still expected to be asked about skills and reliability.

"Good, because I do not like store-bought hummus. I want it freshly made."

"Fresh is always better."

"Why do you want this job?"

The million-dollar question every employer always asked and Jane never knew how to answer it. To be honest she needed the money but she couldn't say that at an interview.

"I believe there are skills that I could learn in this position that would benefit me later in life, and I am looking for a fresh start. I would like to broaden my horizons," she replied. Sheikh Asaad raised his eyebrows.

"There's not much you can learn from cooking and cleaning," he said bluntly.

"You can learn something in every job."

"It's not about the money?"

"That is a bonus." It was definitely about the money but Jane did not want to sound like an opportunist.

"Your hair is coming loose," he pointed out.

Jane refrained from frowning at him and pushed back a stray lock of hair. "It's naturally quite wavy," she replied. "But I will keep it under control."

"I see," he replied. "What skills can you bring to this position?" he asked.

Jane talked about how responsible, punctual, reliable, hardworking and good at communicating she was. She talked about how she would be a good fit for the position but it did not seem like the sheikh was paying attention.

"I sometimes entertain a lot of guests. Can you cook for and serve large parties?" he asked.

"Yes, I can, with a little help from other staff members," she replied.

"You would need to learn how to set the table."

Jane immediately knew that Mariam had told him about her not knowing about cutlery.

"Yes, I will learn and make sure not to make mistakes. You can count on me to do my best," she replied with a smile.

"How old are you?" he asked, completely taking a 180-degree turn from the conversation.

"Twenty-five," Jane replied.

"You are not married." He looked at her empty right hand.

"No, not yet." Jane wondered why he was asking her. The question mark in her mind must have shown on her face because he answered her silent question.

"You are at the marital age," he said.

"There is no marital age. It is whenever one pleases."

"It's so typical of Western women."

"To do what?" Jane raised her eyebrows. That had not sounded polite and it wasn't professional. It was as if he wasn't interested in asking standard interview questions. It was more like he was trying to get a feel of who she was, which was fine but making a comment about Western women was a bit lewd.

"To not marry early, living a wild lifestyle, not taking on wifely duties," he said so calmly as if he was saying something pleasant. Jane's jaw hung open.

"It's unfair to generalize a population like that," she said. Sheikh Asaad shrugged his shoulders. He seemed so unbothered.

"That is the experience I've had," he replied. Jane had more to say but she wanted the job. She knew that she had to curb her words.

"Do you have more questions to ask me? Regarding the position," she said.

"No, thank you for coming," he said plainly. Jane could tell that she had not gotten the job. She rose to her feet.

"There's nothing wrong with not wanting to marry early or living the way you want," she said.

She turned and headed for the door. As she walked out of the room, the door handle caught her blouse and she stumbled backwards. Jane cursed her breath as she unhinged her blouse from the door handle. She did not even dare to turn around.

Jane confidently walked out and away from the office even though she was dying from embarrassment on the inside.

Chapter 2

Jane

"Sorry?" Jane said. She was not sure what she had heard Mariam say. Jane increased the volume on her phone.

"You got the job, you start tomorrow," said Mariam.

Jane couldn't believe what she was hearing. Her interview had progressed poorly. The sheikh barely asked professional questions. He had talked about her hair and the fact that she was unwed. As a result, she had lashed out at him before she left. It didn't make sense that he had given her the job and wanted her to start so soon.

"I don't understand. He actually wants to hire me?" Jane needed to hear it one more time so that she would be convinced that she wasn't crazy.

"Apparently," Mariam replied coldly. "Are you going to take the job or not?"

"Yeah, I guess I will." Even though Jane did not understand how she had gotten the job, she was not going to turn it down. The money was good.

"You need to arrive at 5 o'clock tomorrow and not a second later. The sheikh dislikes tardiness," she said.

"I'll be on time."

"Good. You will be working 5-9 p.m. on Fridays, 12-7 p.m. on Saturdays and Sundays."

"Okay." The hours were good for Jane because she had classes on Monday, Tuesday and Wednesday.

"Do you have any questions?"

"None at the moment."

"I will see you tomorrow."

"Okay, bye."

Regina unlocked the front door and walked into the apartment as Jane hung up. "Who was that?" Regina asked as she put the grocery bags on the floor. She turned and shut the front door. Jane sprang to her feet.

"You won't believe it," she said.

"Who?"

"Mariam, Sheikh Asaad's secretary."

"You got the job?" Regina's eyes widened.

"Yeah, I did." Jane smiled and nodded.

"Congratulations!" Regina let out a squeak in excitement.

"I just can't believe it."

"He must have liked you."

Jane laughed sarcastically. "Not a chance," she said. She picked up the grocery bags and headed to the kitchen with them.

"Are you making dinner?" Regina shouted behind her. "Start preparing for the sheikh!"

Jane laughed as she walked into the kitchen, it was more of a nervous laugh. She wanted the job and she knew that she was a great cook but cooking Arabic food was completely different. She was also nervous about working for the sheikh. He seemed like he was a tough man to please, judging from Mariam's words and from her first meeting with him.

***

Jane arrived at Sheikh Asaad's home at 4:50 p.m. She had made a conscious effort to be early. She showed up dressed in a pair of slim-fit formal trousers and a shirt. She wanted to look smart and professional.

"Thank you for coming early," Mariam said to Jane as she walked through the front door.

"I am happy to be here," Jane replied.

"Please follow me."

Jane nodded and followed Mariam down the hallway. Mariam gave Jane a tour of the house. They first went to the sheikh's office. Keeping his office clean was going to be one of Jane's duties.

"The sheikh keeps his paperwork in a specific order. So when you clean, it is important not to move things around," Mariam said to Jane.

"I will keep everything in its place," Jane replied.

They exited the office and headed to the kitchen. Jane was just in awe of the kitchen. Her kitchen would fit into his kitchen at least eight times. The floors and countertops were made of black marble. The cabinets were white. There were high leather stools at the island in the middle of the kitchen. A silver chandelier hung above the island.

"Always put the food into porcelain bowls and allow the sheikh to dish the food onto the plate for himself," said Mariam.

"Okay?" Jane's answer sounded more like a question than an answer.

"He is particular about his portions."

Suddenly the sheikh walked into the kitchen. Jane had forgotten how authoritative his presence was. He was so tall and muscular; it was hard not to notice his presence. His stubble had grown a bit more.

"Good evening, Sheikh Asaad," Mariam greeted him with a bow.

"Good evening," Jane greeted him. She was not sure if she was meant to bow also. She felt quite awkward because of how they had left things. She had not expected to see him after the interview.

"You are on time," he said to Jane as he checked his watch. Jane slightly crossed her eyebrows. It was as if he had expected her to be late.

"Yes sir," she replied.

"You can start on the dinner after you get changed."

"Changed?"

"Of course. All my staff has to wear a uniform."

Uniform? The word echoed in Jane's head. The idea of wearing a uniform was so outdated to her. He had taken her by surprise.

"I hadn't given it to her yet. I will go get it now," said Mariam. She quickly walked out of the room.

"You will wear white, and your uniform must stay clean," said Sheikh Asaad.

"It will be hard to clean the house in white and stay clean," Jane replied.

"It's a measure of cleanliness. I can't stand dirty employees. Things happen, if you get messy then you will change immediately."

Jane was getting the idea that the sheikh was a clean freak. People like that were hard to please, they practically went over everything with a white glove. Fortunately for Jane, she was tidy by nature.

"Very well, sir. What shall I cook for you?" Jane asked.

"We'll start simply," he said calmly. "A well-done steak and Mediterranean salad. Use olive oil instead of mayonnaise for the salad."

"Yes sir." That was simple, Jane thought to herself. Mariam walked into the room with a white skirt and white blouse. She handed the clothes to Jane.

"Thank you, I will go get changed now." Jane took a few steps towards the door and came to a halt when she realized that she did not know where to get changed. She turned to face Mariam.

"Down the hall, last door on the right," Mariam said before Jane even asked.

"Thank you," Jane walked out of the kitchen and went to get changed.

She gasped as she walked into the bathroom. It was of moderate size but it was gorgeous. The floors were white marble. The sink was glass, and the taps were gold. The toilet had an option to wash your bottom. It made Jane giggle like a schoolchild.

There was even a golden chandelier in the bathroom. Jane had never seen so many in one house. She quickly undressed and got changed into her uniform. She checked herself in the mirror by the sink. The skirt was slightly loose on her. She did not have the wide hips to fill it.

Jane sighed and stuffed her clothes into her handbag. She left the bathroom and returned to the kitchen.

"The uniform fits you just fine," Mariam said as Jane re-entered the kitchen.

"Yes." Jane smiled.

"I am leaving now. Do you have any questions before I go?"

"You are leaving?" Jane raised her eyebrows. She expected Mariam to be there for her entire shift.

"The sheikh needs me on another matter," she replied. Jane nodded. Mariam wasn't all that friendly but she did not want to be left alone. The first day of anything always sucked for Jane. She hated the first day of school or work.

"On the days that I do work, do I work alone?" Jane asked Mariam.

"There will be other maids, and they have retired for the day now. So you just clean your designated areas which are the sheikh's office, his bedroom, balcony and gym," Mariam replied.

Jane raised her eyebrows. She still hadn't been shown those areas yet. "Alright," she said.

"On Friday, you are responsible for dinner. On Saturday and Sunday, the chef only does the breakfast. You will cook the lunch and dinner," she said. Jane nodded. "Any other questions?" Mariam asked.

"No."

"Okay, I shall take my leave." Mariam walked out and left Jane in the kitchen.

Jane started opening drawers in search of an apron. She was used to cooking without one but she had to keep her uniform clean. She opened the fridge and fished out the ingredients that she needed.

Just as she was marinating the steak, she realized that she had not asked the sheikh what kind of spices he liked. She suddenly felt flustered. She did not know whether she was to ask him or not. She tilted her head back and cursed in frustration. She decided to use a little bit of *ras el hanout* since it was a famous Arabic spice. She hoped that Sheikh Asaad would like it. After marinating it, Jane put the steak on the grill. Then she prepared the salad.

Jane searched for instructions on how to set the table on the internet. It was ridiculous that she had not learned how to set the table before her shift but she had not bothered to learn when she thought that she was not getting the job. Thankfully Google existed. She set the table per Google's instructions. She did not want anything to go wrong on her first day. It was a miracle that she had even gotten the job.

The Brazilian wooden table in the dining room was large enough to fit a party of fifteen. She placed the plate and cutlery at the head of the table. When Jane was finished cooking and setting the table, she went to Sheikh Asaad's office to let him know that the food was ready. She knocked on his door and waited for his permission to enter.

"You may enter," he called out.

"Sheikh Asaad, the food is ready," she said. He looked up from his paperwork.

"I'll be there in two minutes."

"Yes sir." She turned on her heel.

"Be careful with the door handle."

Jane's eyes flew wide open. He was referring to when she had her interview. She had tried to leave in a rush but her blouse got caught on the door handle. It was embarrassing and she did not need him to bring it up.

"Thank you." For reminding me about that embarrassing moment, you jerk, she finished off the sentence in her head as she walked off.

Chapter 3

Fadi

Sheikh Fadi Asaad walked into his dining room where Jane waited for him. He sat down and scanned the table. She had set the cutlery correctly. Last he had heard from Mariam, she did not know how to set the table. At least she had learned now. Jane left the room and returned with his food. He watched her as she walked into the room and served his food.

She was tall, possibly five feet seven inches. She had a small figure, small hips and a small chest. Her brown hair had a few subtle golden streaks. Her big blue eyes were intriguing. She had medium-sized pink lips.

"Can I get you anything else?" she asked.

"No," Fadi replied. She nodded and headed for the exit. "Mariam must not have told you."

Jane turned around. "Told me what?" she asked.

"You have to stand by the door whilst I eat."

Jane slowly widened her eyes. Her reaction amused Fadi. He wanted to laugh but he did not.

"I do?" she asked.

"Yes, just in case I need anything else."

Jane cleared her throat. "Okay," she said and stood by the door. It was such an old custom that royal and noble families still followed. She probably thought he was strange, especially since she did not have any experience working as a maid.

Fadi looked at his food. It looked appetizing. He picked up his knife and cut into his meat. He took a bite and chewed slowly. The steak was flavored with ras el hanout spice. He raised his eyebrows and looked at her.

"You used ras el hanout," he said. Jane looked at him and nodded.

"I did. I was not sure how you liked your steak," she replied.

"Salt and pepper, or cumin or plain but served with hummus."

"I'll remember for next time. Does this one taste bad?"

"No." It actually tasted good. He had always found that Western chefs did not use the Arabic spice very well. It was either too little or too much or they mixed it with other spices which resulted in a complicated taste.

"Okay," she replied.

Fadi kept eating his food. There was silence in the room for a little while.

"Sheikh," said Jane.

"Yes," Fadi replied.

"Why did you hire me?"

"Are you regretting your decision to take the job?"

"No, I am grateful."

"But?"

"I am confused." She cleared her throat. "I did not think that the interview went well."

Fadi raised his eyebrows. The interview had been rather interesting for him. No one had ever raised their voice at him especially in an interview. He was intrigued by her. He wanted to see what kind of a woman she was.

"I thought it was fine," he replied. Jane raised her eyebrows.

"Um, okay." She was unconvinced. Fadi finished up his dinner. He picked up the white napkin and wiped his mouth.

"Clear the table," he said to Jane. She approached the table and took the plates and cutlery. Fadi noticed that she cleaned the table from his left instead of his right side. She had a lot to learn.

"Come back here when you have finished clearing the table," said Fadi.

"Yes sir," Jane replied. She cleared the table and then returned to the dining room as Fadi had instructed. He rose from the chair.

"Follow me," he ordered.

Fadi walked out of the dining room and headed down the hallway. Jane followed behind him quietly. He headed up the stairs. When they reached the top of the stairs, Fadi followed the wide corridor. When they came to an end, there were white double doors. There was a white door with a golden handle to the right, leading to another room. Fadi took the door to the right.

They walked into a moderately sized air-conditioned room filled with exercise equipment. Fadi stopped in the middle of the room. He slid his hands in his pockets and turned to face to Jane.

"As you can see, this is my gym," he said to her. "I will need you to keep it clean and tidy."

"Okay," she replied. Jane looked around the room with fascination etched on her face.

"You don't work out?" he asked her. It was more of a statement than a question. From how her figure was shaped, he could already tell that she did not work to build her muscles.

"No." Jane laughed. "It's too much effort."

"You should."

Jane dropped her jaw. Fadi said nothing. He just headed for the exit. He walked out of the room and slid the double doors open. They walked into a large bedroom with a white marble floor. There was a large bed with a tufted white headboard and grey silk covers at the far end of the room. French double doors led to a balcony to the left side of the room. There was a white door with a golden handle to the right side of the bed leading to the bathroom.

"You favor the color white," Jane pointed out.

"You are to keep this room clean and tidy. Sheets are to be changed every day," Fadi said to her.

"Every day?"

"The days that you are here. On the other days, I have other maids to do that."

"Wow."

"Problem?"

"You're really into cleanliness."

"As people should be. I can't stand a slob."

Jane smiled at him. Her smile seemed as though she was hiding something. She must have wanted to comment on his statement but decided not to. Fadi decided to ignore her. He gestured with his hand towards white double doors at the other end of the room.

"That is my closet," he said. Jane immediately walked over and slid the doors open.

"Everything is arranged according to its color," she called out to him.

"You are to keep it that way."

There was silence for a moment. "I will," she said to him.

"I assume Mariam has told you what days and times you will be working," he said.

"She did."

"Make sure you are not late."

"Yes sir."

"She will e-mail you a list of foods I like to eat and do not like to eat, and recipes. Since you know how to cook, it should be no issue following the recipes."

"It'll be fine."

"You may go downstairs and do the dishes. Make sure you hand-wash them. Dishwashers do not always remove everything."

"Okay," Jane replied. She turned on her heel and left the room.

Fadi watched Jane walk out of the room before he started getting undressed. He noticed that she had impulsive speech. She was not one to bite her tongue. He had never met a woman like that. Women and men always agreed with what he said. They never challenged him nor did they express their opinions unless he asked for them.

He went to his bathroom and got into his stone-tiled shower and switched on the water. He let the warm water run down his body. After he finished showering, he dried off with a white towel. He slipped into loose slacks and a polo shirt. He went back to his office. He still had some work to do.

Around nine, Jane knocked on his door. "Come in," he called out to her. She walked into the room and stood in front of his desk.

"I have finished for the day," she said to him.

"You may go home."

"I will see you tomorrow."

Fadi nodded. As she turned, her hip hit the corner of his desk. "Ow," she said quietly. Fadi just stared at her with his eyebrows raised. She did not even turn around; she just walked out of the room as if nothing had happened. No doubt she was embarrassed.

Chapter 4

Jane

"What are you wearing?" Regina asked Jane as she walked through the front door of their apartment.

"My uniform," Jane replied. She took her shoes off and headed to the kitchen. It had been at least four hours since she had eaten. She switched on the stove and cooked some seafood ramen. Her mother hated that she ate instant noodles a lot and always told her to eat balanced meals.

Jane poured her ramen in a bowl and went to the living room where Regina sat watching television.

"Noodles," Regina commented.

"I'm too hungry to wait for a full meal." She shoved a forkful of noodles in her mouth.

"How was work?"

"Awkward."

"How so?"

"It's awkward when you are new and you don't know anything." It was worse because she was working alone.

"I've always wondered what sheikhs were like." Regina looked quite curious. Jane swallowed her noodles before she answered.

"I wonder too. It's still too early to say what Sheikh Asaad is like," Jane replied. The only thing she had concluded was that he was very smart.

Regina pulled her phone out of her pocket and swiped the screen. "What's his last name?" Regina asked her.

"Asaad," Jane replied. She looked up from her food and turned her attention to Regina. "What are you doing?"

"Looking for him on Google."

"Why?"

"Don't you want to know about the person you are working for?"

"That's if he is online."

"He sounds rich enough to be."

Jane finished eating and put her bowl down on the coffee table. She sighed with satisfaction. Now that she was full, she had to go study. Her master's was challenging but in a good way. She was enjoying it.

"Fadi Asaad." Regina gasped. "He is handsome. Is this him?" Regina turned her phone to show Jane the screen.

"Yes," Jane replied.

"Oh wow." Regina swiped the screen. "He's from Al Hamri."

"Really?" Jane knew about the country because of her classes at the university. She had learned that the country was the biggest oil provider in the Middle East. Regina nodded.

"It says that his family owns an oil company," said Regina.

"How old is he?"

"Twenty-nine."

He was only four years older than her. She had not seen a ring on his finger and there were no traces of a wife in his home. "He's not married?" Jane asked Regina.

"No, he is not," she replied. Jane shook her head as she rose to her feet. He had judged her on not being married and yet he was unwed himself.

"I'm going to study," Jane said as she picked up her bowl. She was not all that interested in learning about the sheikh.

"Wait, we are still stalking the sheikh," said Regina. Jane burst into laughter.

"Not we but you," she said.

"He has a younger brother and a younger sister."

"Bye, Regina." Jane headed for her room. Regina smiled and waved at her.

***

Jane arrived at work a couple of minutes early. Mariam and the sheikh had both emphasized that she was to be on time. Jane felt as though the sheikh would fire her if she was late. Mariam was waiting for her in the drawing room. The furniture was pale grey and white. There were large windows.

"Hi," Jane greeted her as she walked into the room.

"Hello, please have a seat," Mariam replied and motioned towards the seat opposite her. Mariam was dressed in a cream pencil skirt and a beige blouse. She wore red-soled Christian Louboutin high heels.

"What's this room?" Jane asked Mariam.

"The drawing room," she replied.

"I never quite understood the difference between a drawing room and a living room," said Jane. Mariam looked at Jane as though she had asked a dumb question.

"It's mainly for the reception of guests."

The answer wasn't convincing enough to Jane. A drawing room and a living room served the same purpose. The only difference was that there was no television in the drawing room.

"Okay." Jane smiled and nodded.

"Have you looked at the recipes I sent you?"

"Yes, I have. Thank you for sending them."

"The chef is not yet off duty. I can ask him to stay longer and help you cook."

"I will be okay. At least now I know what the sheikh does not like to eat."

"Very well." Mariam handed Jane some documents. "Please fill in your bank details and Social Security number. This is so we can pay you."

"Sure." Jane took the paperwork. She filled in her full name, address, Social Security number and bank details. She then handed the paperwork back to Mariam.

"You will get paid fortnightly."

"That's fine."

"If you need to use the bathroom, you may use the ones downstairs."

Jane nodded in response. She got an unfriendly vibe from Mariam. She was not warm towards her. Jane couldn't understand why but she decided to brush it off. Mariam rose to her feet.

"I am taking my leave," she said. Jane also stood up.

"Alright, take care," she said. Mariam nodded and left the room. Jane was already dressed in her uniform. She headed to the kitchen. She was to serve the sheikh his lunch in an hour. She met the chef on his way out of the kitchen. She smiled and greeted him.

"I can do this," Jane said to herself. She went to the fridge and pulled out turkey breast. Judging from the list Mariam had emailed her, the sheikh liked healthy foods. The list contained lean meats, fruits, vegetables, healthy smoothies and salads. It made sense that he would have a gym in his home.

After Jane was finished cooking, she went to look for the sheikh. He was not in his office, so she went upstairs to look for him. She ran into one of the maids in the corridor. "Hi, I'm Jane," she introduced herself.

"Hello, I'm Rania," the maid replied.

"I am the new maid that will be working weekends."

"Nice to meet you."

"Was there a previous maid before me or did he just need an extra maid?"

Jane wondered why the sheikh wanted to hire an additional maid, when he already had many working for him. He could easily have asked them to share the duties.

"As you will come to learn, Sheikh Asaad likes his house to be very clean," said Rania. Jane smiled and nodded. She had already learned that he was a clean freak.

"He is quite particular about his office and bedroom, so he wanted to hire someone to clean those specific areas. He would rather have a hundred people work here than ten if it means an extra-clean house," Rania continued. Jane raised an eyebrow.

"I see. I guess I better do a good job." Jane smiled.

"Yes, you do not want to cross him. He can be quite short-tempered."

"Thanks for the heads-up. Have you seen him?"

"He is in the gym."

"Thanks. See you around." Jane walked off. She continued down the corridor until she had reached the entrance of the gym. She knocked on the door before she walked in. Sheikh Asaad was by the free weights pumping some heavy-looking weights. He wore a white T-shirt and grey shorts.

His gym attire revealed his muscular physique. Jane could not help but stand and stare. He looked so attractive and manly. Part of her wanted to stand there for much longer and just admire his beauty. The other part of her wanted to dash out of the room before he noticed her. Knowing her luck, she would probably knock something over on her way out.

"You need something?" the sheikh asked without looking at her. His attention was on the weights in his hands.

"Me?" Jane asked. That was the first thing that came out of her mouth. She felt embarrassed about being caught staring. He had his left shoulder facing the door and there was music playing in the room. Jane thought her presence had not been detected but she was wrong.

"Who else is in this room?" he asked.

"You," she said. Sheikh Asaad turned his head to face her. She laughed awkwardly. "That was a joke." She cleared her throat. So inappropriate, she said to herself. She instantly regretted the joke.

"I have finished preparing lunch. I was coming to call you," said Jane in her most professional tone.

"I will come once I have showered," he replied. His tone was unchanged. It did not seem like he was annoyed by her words.

"Yes sir." Jane scurried out of the room and shut the door behind her. She smacked her forehead with her palm.

"Good going, Jane," she said to herself sarcastically. Her mother had always warned her about her quick tongue. She did not need to say everything that entered her brain. She sighed and walked off.

The sheikh came downstairs about half an hour later. He had changed into a pair of khaki shorts and a black T-shirt. Jane noticed how athletic his legs were. He had muscular calves. He had a good balance of skin and hair. A lot of men were either too hairy or hairless. The sheikh had just the right amount of hair.

Jane could tell that he had showered because his hair was still wet. She quickly served his lunch. She wished she could just sit in the kitchen while he ate. She did not like having to stand in the room while he ate. It was such an old custom. She could not believe that he followed it.

"I will need you to clean the gym and restack the weights after you are finished cleaning the kitchen," Sheikh Asaad said to Jane.

"Yes sir," she replied. He slowly looked at her from head to toe and then back up to her head. Jane felt so awkward.

"Just clean the gym. I'll restack the weights."

"Sir?"

"You don't look as though you have the strength for it."

"Excuse me?"

"You have weak arms."

"I do not!" she protested. She did not appreciate his assumptions. He looked at her with an expression as if he was asking her if she was sure about that. "I can handle the weights. I'll be fine," she added. The sheikh said nothing. He just returned his attention to his food and kept eating.

Jane cleared the table when he finished eating. Sheikh Asaad just rose from the table and walked out of the room. Jane felt slightly annoyed because he had not thanked her. He just left the room. He could at least say excuse me or something polite. For $3,000 a month, though, Jane was going to have to put up with anything the sheikh did or said to her.

After cleaning up, she went to clean his gym. She approached the free weights with contempt. She could handle putting them back in their places. How could the sheikh say she was too weak to do it? She crouched down to pick up the heaviest-looking dumbbell. Her eyes almost popped out of their sockets when she couldn't pick it up.

Jane scrunched up her skirt and took a deep breath. She refused to be defeated. She crouched down again and attempted to lift the dumbbell. She managed to get it a few inches off the floor but no more.

"Do you want to give yourself a hernia?" she heard Sheikh Asaad's voice. He approached her and took the weight from her. He carried it as though it weighed nothing.

"I was going to lift it," she said.

"You were going to injure yourself." He returned the rest of the weights to their places. Jane picked up a clean rag and started wiping the machines.

"You need to train your arms," Sheikh Asaad said to her.

"My arms are fine."

"For a fifteen-year-old."

Jane looked at him with a frown on her face. She could feel herself getting annoyed at him. She was already embarrassed and now he continued to taunt her about it.

"Was there anything else that I could do for you?" she asked him. The sheikh slid his hands in his pockets with a smirk on his face.

"No." He turned and left the room. Jane huffed. She could not believe him. He was such a meanie. She returned her attention to the treadmill and continued to clean it with her cleaning rag.

Chapter 5

Fadi

Fadi smirked as he walked out of the gym. He was amused by Jane. He knew that she was not strong enough to lift the dumbbells but she was stubborn about it. She had struggled with the dumbbell and he had walked in on that moment. She needed some strength training.

He went to his home office to get some work done. Others relaxed during the weekend but he used that time to work. He was going to take over the oil company once his father retired. He wanted to be the type of owner that knew everything about the business in and out. He was quite particular and hands-on with everything.

Later that night, Fadi took a shower and changed into a pair of brown trousers and a white shirt. He brushed his black curls. Fadi took pride in his appearance. He made sure to always look smart and smell good. He headed to the kitchen where Jane was.

"I haven't finished cooking yet," she said to him. Fadi shrugged his shoulders.

"I am going out for dinner," he said lazily. Jane narrowed her gaze at him. She couldn't hide her annoyance; it was either that or she was not trying to hide it.

"So you will not be eating here?"

"If I am going out for dinner, it means that I will not eat here. Naturally."

Jane placed her small fists on her hips. She looked at the pot on the stove and sighed. Fadi walked over to the refrigerator and opened it. He took out a bottle of water and took a sip.

"Take the food with you," he said to her. Jane looked at him and crossed her eyebrows.

"I can just put it in the fridge and you could eat it tomorrow," she said. Fadi shook his head.

"I do not like eating food that has been cooked a day before."

She opened her mouth as if she was going to say something, and then she closed it. She cleared her throat twice before she spoke.

"Sir," she said. "If you do not wish to eat at home, could you please let me know in advance?"

Fadi slowly raised his eyebrows. He was both amused and shocked by her boldness. His other staff would have just said yes sheikh. They never expressed their ill feelings or disappointment to him. In that moment, Fadi could tell that Jane wanted to tell him off for his last-minute decision.

"Don't be late tomorrow." Fadi turned on his heel and exited. If he needed to leave at a moment's notice, then it was well within his rights.

***

"Good evening, Sheikh Asaad." A maid greeted Fadi as she opened the door for him. He had gone to his friend's house for dinner. The maid had the biggest smile across her face.

"Where is Sofian?" he asked her.

"He is waiting for you in his dining room," she said. "Right this way." She led Fadi to the dining room.

"Sheikh Asaad," Sofian said as Fadi walked in. Sofian was Fadi's oldest friend.

"Hello Sofian," Fadi replied as he pulled out a chair. He joined Sofian at the table. His maids filed into the room with trays of different foods. They talked business as they ate their dinner.

"What else is new with you? You invest too much of your time in business. You need a social life," he said. Fadi leaned back into his chair and took a sip of his drink.

"There is nothing new in my life," he replied.

"Wow. My friend, you have a boring life."

Fadi chuckled a little bit. "I have a new maid," he said. Sofian burst into laughter.

"That's it?"

"I don't like change."

"You are a caveman."

"I am set in my ways, and it works for me," said Fadi. Sofian shook his head.

"Well, this maid of yours, is she pretty at least?" Sofian asked. Fadi crossed his eyebrows as he thought about his answer. After a long pause, he finally answered.

"She is, but more than that, she is interesting," he said. "She's a feisty one. She gave me a piece of her mind at the end of her interview." Fadi told Sofian about his interview with Jane. Sofian responded with a loud chuckle.

"And yet you still hired her?" Sofian asked.

"I did."

"You let a random woman speak to you like that and then you hired her? That is unlike you."

"She intrigues me," he said. Jane was an intriguing woman. He was interested to see more of her feistiness.

***

Jane

Jane dumped the cardboard boxes of food onto her kitchen counter. Regina stared at the food in confusion. She looked up at her friend. "Where did you get this food?" she asked. Jane placed her hands on her waist.

"Fadi decided to go out for dinner after I had already started cooking," Jane said. She was still annoyed about that. He had been so unapologetic about it.

"What?" Regina laughed a little.

"Then he told me to take the food home."

"Why?"

"Apparently, he's too good for reheated food," Jane huffed as she opened the cabinets and pulled out some plates.

"Oh, he is one of those people that like to eat food straight after it's been cooked."

"Yes." Jane put the plates on the kitchen counter. "Well, I was not going to let the food go to waste."

"Rich people." Regina shook her head. "But we can forgive him, since he's so handsome."

"I absolutely embarrassed myself in front of him today." Jane opened a drawer and fished out two forks. She handed one to Regina.

"What happened?" Regina asked with eyes full of curiosity. Jane sighed before she relived the horror that had occurred in the gym. Regina gasped before she burst into laughter. She threw her head backwards and laughed even harder. Jane scrunched her eyebrows.

"Okay, Gina, it's not that funny," she complained.

"It is a bit," Regina said between giggles. Jane leveled her gaze at her and waited for her to stop laughing. "But Jane, you know that you aren't particularly strong. Why would you lie about being able to lift the dumbbells?" Regina continued.

Jane shrugged her shoulders. "He had already assumed that I wasn't going to be able to lift them. I did not want to prove him right."

"Then he walked in on your struggle and then he was proved right anyway."

Jane scooped some rice and lamb out of the box onto her plate. She started eating. She groaned at the delicious taste of the food. Fadi was missing out. Part of her hoped that he ate horrible food or got food poisoning. She needed karma to play its part.

"If my boss was half as good-looking as Fadi is, I would not care about what he said or did," said Regina. She worked at a call center. Jane sighed.

"It is my first weekend. Maybe things will change." Jane was not convinced by her own words. She had a feeling that he was always going to be so unfriendly and arrogant towards her. It made her wonder why he even hired her in the first place.

Fortunately, Sunday was uneventful. Jane went to work and did her chores. Fadi had been busy in his office. Jane walked past his office a few times. She wondered what he was doing in there. For most people, Sundays were meant for church or relaxing and not for work.

When it was time for lunch, Jane served Fadi his food. There hadn't been much exchange between them. Jane had hoped for an apology but that had not happened. Fadi ate his food and left the dining room. The same thing happened at dinner. Jane just cleaned up and left for the day.

Chapter 6

Jane

Friday came much sooner than Jane had wanted. She dressed in her so-called uniform and headed to work. She hated having to wear a skirt at work, a white one at that. Skirts were not her style. She preferred to wear trousers. She even preferred to wear dresses rather than skirts.

She arrived at work promptly. Fadi was standing at the front speaking with another man. Fadi was dressed in a pair of black trousers, a crisp white shirt and a black trench coat. It was unbuttoned. He looked like a model in a fashion catalogue, a muscular one. His three-day stubble complemented his strong jaw. The man he was talking to was a head shorter than Fadi. He wore a grey shirt and black trousers.

As Jane got closer to them, she could hear that they were talking about machinery. The smaller man was reporting to Fadi about a fault in machinery.

"Thomilson Drills provides terrible machinery," said Jane as she walked past them.

"Stop," Fadi's deep and commanding voice sounded from behind Jane. She had her hand on the doorknob, ready to walk into the house. She stopped and turned around.

"Sir?" she said.

"What are you talking about?" He looked so shocked.

"Thomilson Drills has terrible machinery," she repeated.

"Elaborate."

"Their machines boast a lot of speed but they have a poor flow system and the motor is horrible." Jane crossed her arms over her chest. "Dallas Oils has the best machines for drilling. Their motors will last longer," she added.

Fadi's eyebrows were raised so high, they were almost one with his hairline. "You just happen to know this?" he asked her.

"No. I'm doing my master's in petroleum refining systems at MIT," she said.

"Really?"

"Yes." Jane nodded. Fadi stared at Jane for a moment. It was clear that he was really shocked. He turned his head and looked at the other man.

"Why were you not aware of this?" Fadi asked him.

"My apologies, sheikh. Thomilson Drills had great reviews," the man replied. He looked at Jane with displeasure on his face. Jane played with her fingers. It wasn't her intention to get him into trouble with the sheikh.

"Clearly not. Their machinery is not great."

"Their machines were within our budget."

Fadi looked at him as though he had lost his mind. "It's not as if we do not have enough money to buy the best machinery. Quality over price. ALWAYS!" Fadi raised his voice a little. He was angry and it was obvious.

"Yes sheikh. We will order better drills," the man replied. Fadi was standing there with his hands in his pockets looking down at the other man, since he was taller. The other man looked intimidated. Of course he was. Fadi was bigger and scarier. But Jane wasn't scared. She found him attractive in that moment and cursed herself when she remembered that he was a rude man.

"If you had thoroughly researched the company before purchasing from them, we would not have this issue," said Fadi.

"It will not happen again," the man replied.

"Of course it will not. Otherwise you will find yourself without a job."

Jane's eyebrows shot up. "I did not mean for things to escalate this far," she said.

"I am really sorry, shei–" Before the man could finish his sentence, Fadi cut him off with a raise of his hand.

"You may leave," Fadi dismissed him with his hand. The man bowed his head before he walked off. Jane stood there awkwardly. She only wanted to help but instead she made things worse for the other man.

"Sorry!" she called out after him.

"It's his own fault for not doing his job properly," Fadi said to Jane.

"Mmm. I will just go start work now." She turned on her heel as she was ready to disappear from Fadi's sight. One of the maids had already warned her about his impulse to fire people. Fadi surprised her when he reached for the door handle and opened the door for her.

"I did not know that you study petroleum refining," Fadi said to her.

"Thank you." Jane walked through the front door. "You don't know because we never discussed it," she added. He had never taken the time to speak to her, so of course he would not know about her. Even at the interview, he did not ask about her education history.

Fadi grunted. "Interesting," he said.

"I know that I am an interesting woman."

Fadi raised his eyebrows. "I meant that your career choice is interesting," he said. Jane narrowed her gaze.

Fadi always knew how to make her feel awkward and shy.

"My choices and I are interesting." She tucked stray lock of hair behind her ear. Fadi touched Jane's arm. She stopped walking and turned to face him. She jerked her head backwards when she realized just how close he was to her.

"Why are you working here?" he asked her.

"Sorry?" Jane asked.

"Why aren't you working for an oil company?"

"Oh, that is because the companies want someone with experience and someone that can work full-time. Because I am still doing my master's, I can't commit to full-time hours."

Fadi was looking at her with an expressionless face. His face was so handsome. It had to be illegal to look that good. Jane could smell him. He smelled so good. It made him even more attractive, if that was possible.

"That's a shame," he replied.

"It is but it's okay. Hopefully I get something after my master's."

Fadi said nothing. He just slipped his hands in his pockets and turned on his heel. Jane's jaw hung open as she watched him walk away. She was pretty sure that they hadn't finished talking. Even if he felt that they were finished, he should have at least said he was leaving or something.

"Sheikh Asaad." She cleared her throat. He stopped walking and turned his head.

"What?" he replied.

"We were still in the middle of a conversation." She was not going to stand by idly and allow him to just walk off in the middle of a conversation. He may have been her boss and a sheikh but that did not give him the right to be that rude. She had just witnessed someone almost getting fired, so she knew she was taking a risk calling him out on his rudeness.

"There was nothing more to say," he replied.

"Even so, wouldn't you at least say that you are heading off, or bye or something?" She could hear herself raising her voice. Jane cleared her throat and clasped her fingers together. For sure she was about to get fired.

Fadi raised his eyebrows slowly. He looked more amused than annoyed. "Shall I ask for permission to leave?" he asked her. Jane narrowed her gaze.

"That is not what I meant," she said quietly.

"Get to work." Fadi walked off. Jane sighed with relief. She thought that he was going to fire her or yell at her but he did neither. He looked amused. He was a man full of surprises.

Jane put her apron on when she walked in the kitchen. She started on the cooking. It was already past six and she needed to make dinner for the sheikh. Fortunately for her, Friday shifts were only four hours long. She only needed to make dinner and clean up.

After she was finished cooking, she set the table and then called the sheikh for dinner. He was in his office as usual. She wondered if he had a social life at all. There had to be more to life than work for him.

Jane had dished the food into porcelain bowls. There were serving spoons on the table. She reluctantly went to stand by the door. She hated doing that. It was quite ridiculous. Fadi leaned back in his chair and looked at Jane.

"Come and serve me," he said to her.

"Sir?" She was pretty sure he preferred to dish out food for himself, well, that was what Mariam had told her.

"My plate is empty."

Jane opened her mouth and then closed it. She opened it again. "I thought you preferred to serve yourself," she said.

"Today I want you do it."

Jane pressed her lips together tightly and slowly walked towards him. She picked up a serving spoon and dished the rice for him. She could sense his dark gaze resting on her as she served him. Being so close to him and having him stare at her like that... dammit, he was making her feel so shy.

Chapter 7

Fadi

Jane was a fascinating woman. Fadi was still shocked to learn that she was studying for her master's degree at MIT. MIT was not a university just anyone could get into. You needed to have the grades. She must be an intelligent girl. He had missed it when hiring her because he wasn't interested in education. He just wanted a smart housemaid to cook and clean for him.

Fadi watched her as she awkwardly served him. She had beautiful porcelain skin and brown hair with just a sparkle of golden highlights. She had big blue eyes. She was very feisty. It was interesting. She always spoke her mind. She never held back her thoughts. No one around him had the guts to do that.

As Jane poured water into the glass for him, her belly rumbled. Her eyes flew wide open for a split second and quickly returned to normal size. She kept on serving as if nothing had happened.

"Are you famished?" he asked her.

"No. I am fine," she replied.

"Then why is your belly rumbling?"

"It's not." Right after she said that, her belly rumbled again. This time it was louder and more intense. Fadi looked at her and raised his eyebrow. Jane cleared her throat. "I am just thirsty," she said.

Fadi rose to his feet. He went to the kitchen and took a dinner plate from the cabinets. He took a fork and knife and then returned to the dining room.

"Sit," he said to Jane as he placed the plate on the table. She opened her mouth to speak but he beat her to it. "Now," he added. Jane slowly sat down to his left. He dished the rice and lamb onto the plate.

"Eat," he said to her. She slowly picked up the fork, with redness creeping into her cheeks.

"I said I was fine," she mumbled. Fadi said nothing in return. He just looked at her in amusement. "Okay, so maybe I am a bit hungry. I was working on an assignment before I came here," she explained.

"What made you choose to study oil and gas engineering?" Fadi picked up his fork and started eating.

"I've always enjoyed math and physics." Jane started eating also, then paused to continue. "I developed an interest in oil and gas in school when we went on a field trip to an oil rig."

"A field trip."

"Yes. It was my prize for making into the top ten at a regional physics competition."

Competition. She was smart enough to take part in regional competitions. He was impressed. Fadi watched Jane eating. She ate as though someone was chasing her.

"You were acting all shy and now you're eating so quickly as if someone is coming to get your food," he said to her. Jane frowned.

"I wasn't shy," she said. She took a serving spoon and dished out more food for herself. Fadi raised his eyebrows.

"You have a large appetite."

"I do." She did not even seem embarrassed about it. All the women he had been around had always been shy about eating a lot of food in his presence. They ate small portions and never took a second plate of food.

"And yet you are slim."

"Fast metabolism."

Fadi grunted in response. They ate the rest of their dinner in silence. When he was finished eating, he rose to his feet. He headed out of the room. He thought Jane would complain about his abrupt exit but she did not. She was probably too busy enjoying her food. Fadi just smiled to himself as he left the room.

The next day, Mariam came over to his house unannounced. Fadi leaned back his chair as she came in.

"Good afternoon, sheikh," she said with a bow.

"What brings you over?" he asked her. She slipped her hand into her bag and fished out a white envelope.

"Here." She handed it to him. Fadi opened the envelope. There was a cream-colored card inside. He opened the card and read it. It was an invitation to a charity dinner. Fadi crossed his eyebrows.

"You could have given it to me on Monday," he said to her. He looked at her and realized that there was more to her visit.

"That is true," she replied. She wore a purple bodycon dress and black heels. She had a curvy figure, unlike Jane. Her jet-black hair was straight, unlike Jane. Jane had wavy hair with a stray lock that added the finishing touch to her feisty persona. Fadi frowned when he realized that he was comparing Mariam to Jane. The real question was why was he was thinking of Jane so much?

"Why are you here, Mariam?" he asked. She cleared her throat and walked around his desk and stood beside him. She reached out and touched his well-defined arm. Fadi raised an eyebrow and looked at her.

"I miss you," she said to him.

"You shouldn't."

"Why not?"

"It was one time, and we agreed to keep it professional." A few months ago, Fadi had made the mistake of sleeping with Mariam. They had talked it over and agreed to keep things professional but she had her moments when she wanted to be with him again. He could tell that for her it had been more than just sex.

"We can separate professional and personal matters," she said.

"I do not think that is wise."

Mariam leaned on his desk, facing him. She gently settled her right hand on Fadi's chest.

"Just once more?" she asked him.

"Mariam, I will not repeat myself. Go home."

Embarrassed, she cleared her throat and stood up straight. "Is it because of her?" she asked.

"Her?" he asked.

"Faiza."

Fadi closed his eyes and took a deep breath. Faiza was the princess of Al Hamri. The king favored Fadi's family because they were one of the most esteemed and powerful families in Al Hamri. Their company was also the largest oil company in the country and their earnings contributed largely to the country's economy. So the king wanted his daughter to marry Fadi.

"It has nothing to do with Faiza," Fadi replied. He just was not attracted to Mariam.

"Then what is it?"

"You are my assistant and I would like to keep it like that."

Mariam looked at him with such disappointment. She sighed deeply. "Okay." Mariam bowed her head and left his office. Fadi sighed. He did not want Mariam to become attached to him. She was the most efficient assistant he had ever had. It would be a shame to let her go. He hoped that she would not become a problem.

Faiza was another problem he had to deal with sooner or later. He was in no rush to get married nor did he want to. However, the marriage had already been arranged and he had no choice but to go through with it. The date had been set to be a day after his thirtieth birthday. That was in five months. The time had come sooner than he wanted.

Chapter 8

Jane

Jane was just about to knock on Fadi's office door when Mariam swung the door open. Jane awkwardly stood there with her fist in the air. Jane smiled. "Hi," she said to Mariam.

"Did you hear what you wanted to hear?" Mariam asked her. Jane frowned.

"Huh? What do you mean?"

"Eavesdropping is a detestable trait." She looked at Jane as though she was the most disgusting thing on earth before she walked off. Jane stood there with her jaw hung open. She wanted to call out to Mariam that she was not eavesdropping but it was already too late. Mariam had stormed off.

"Do you need something?" said Fadi. Jane turned towards his voice. She had forgotten that the office door was still open.

"I was not eavesdropping," she explained. "I had only just arrived and was about to knock."

"What do you want?"

"To clean your office." She suddenly wondered what Mariam and the sheikh had been talking about. Whatever it was had gotten them both so annoyed.

"Come in," Fadi said to her. Jane walked in slowly. She had a basket of cleaning items in her left hand. She placed it on the floor.

"Um, do you prefer for me to come back later or...?" She knew that it was going to be awkward cleaning his office in his presence. She would feel him watching her.

"No," he said. "Go ahead and clean."

"Okay." Jane nodded. Not the answer that she was looking for. Jane walked over to the glass cabinets and decided to start cleaning those. She took out the window cleaner from the basket and a cleaning cloth.

As Jane was cleaning the glass, she turned her head and looked at Fadi. He was focused on some paperwork.

"What is it that you do on the weekends?" The words came out faster than Jane could stop them.

"What is it that you really want to ask me?" Fadi asked. His deep voice rumbled in his throat. It gave Jane goosebumps.

"You seem to work a lot."

Fadi leaned back in his seat and looked at Jane. "You've been watching me," he said. Jane raised her eyebrows.

"Not like that," she spat out. Fadi groaned in response. He did not seem to believe her. Jane turned her attention back to the cabinets to hide how red her cheeks had turned. She had not been watching him. Well, not that much. She had only noticed that he was such a handsome man and had stared at him for long periods of time but that was not watching.

Jane dusted the furniture before she swept the floors. "Would you like to step out for a moment?" she bravely asked Fadi.

"You want me to leave my office?" He looked up from his paperwork. His tone suggested that he thought she had lost her mind.

"Just for a minute. I do not want to get dust on you or anything."

"Come here."

"Excuse me?" Jane raised an eyebrow.

"I want you to look at something."

Jane slowly made her way to his desk. She pulled out the white tufted chair and sat down. "What would you like to show me?" she asked him. Fadi handed her a folder with some documents.

"I need you to make a development plan for this reservoir," he said. Jane gasped.

"Are you sure?" She could barely hide the excitement in her voice.

"I do not say things that I do not mean."

Jane grinned and let out a few giggles. It was going to be her first time making a development plan outside the university. She had only made one as part of an assignment but this, this was the real thing. She was going to make a development plan on her own. It was exciting for her.

"Does it make you that happy?" Fadi asked her. Jane smiled and nodded. "Take it home. Bring it back when you are done. No more than a week."

"But, why would you trust me with this? I am sure you have a bunch of great engineers with PhDs and tons of experience," she said. He had no reason to be trusting her with such an important task. It was a real reservoir, not the made-up models which they used at the university.

He rose from his seat. "Show me how good you are," he said. A challenge. She fully accepted. For some reason, she wanted him to know that she was good. She wanted him to know that she was intelligent and capable.

"Okay," Jane replied.

Fadi slipped his hands into his pockets and walked out of the room.

***

Fadi

Fadi was curious about Jane's ability. She was a student at MIT, studying for her master's. MIT was one of the top universities in the world, especially for engineering. So she was smart. The question was, how smart? Fadi was very much intrigued by her. Not just by her pretty face, but by her feisty personality. She was the only person who dared to speak up to him. He wanted to know more about her.

He was surprised when she returned with the development plan two days later. She wasn't even supposed to work on Monday, and she could have waited until Friday. However, she came on Monday.

"I expected you to take longer," said Fadi.

"Why?" Jane said as she sat down at his desk. She fished out a laptop from her bag.

"I only give people one chance. So you have to give me your best. Are you sure you want to show me right now?" If her calculations were incorrect, then there was no chance of him asking her to do anything for him again.

"You're a bit stingy with chances," she said. Fadi shrugged his shoulders. She flipped her laptop open. "Anyway, here."

Fadi looked at the development plan. She had calculated how deep the reservoir could be dug and how much oil they could expect to find. She had prepared a simple mathematical model illustrating all the information needed.

"I will use this information," said Fadi. Jane raised her eyebrows.

"What?" she asked. She stared at him with her pale face.

"Based on your information, I think it is worth drilling this reservoir."

"Huh." She looked confused. "You want to go on my information?"

"Why not?"

"I did not think you were going to use it."

"What did you think I was trying to do then?"

"I thought this was an old reservoir or something. I don't know. I just did not think that you were going to drill based on my calculations." Jane ran her hand through her hair. Today her hair was not tied up neatly for work. It was in a loose messy ponytail. She wore loose-fitting blue jeans and a white T-shirt.

It was shocking. Most women wore their finest clothes and jewels when they went to meet with Fadi. For them, meeting with Fadi was a chance of a lifetime. Jane dressed as though she was going to the store.

"Where are you coming from?" he asked

"Um, excuse me?" The change in conversation probably shocked her. Fadi was no longer interested in speaking about the reservoir. He thought that she did a good job but she was intent on understanding what he had already explained.

"You are, unkempt," he said. Jane curled her upper lip.

"I look fine."

Fadi raised his eyebrows. He always liked his women smartly dressed and well kempt. Strangely, Jane looked adorable with her hair messy. He imagined that was what her bed hair looked like.

"I am coming from class," she admitted with an eye roll. Fadi let out a laugh.

"Like that?" he said.

"What is wrong with going to class like this? I don't need to dress up for class."

"A woman always needs to take care of her appearance."

She dismissed him with her hand. "My clothes are clean and I smell good," she said.

"And that's enough?"

"Yes."

Fadi said nothing in response. He just raised his eyebrows in amusement. He leaned back in his chair and kept his gaze on her. When she made eye contact with him, her cheeks immediately turned red. She cleared her throat.

"Shall I e-mail this to you then?" she asked. "The development plan."

"Connect your laptop to the printer," he said. She nodded. He watched her every move. He noticed that she bit her bottom lip when she was concentrating on something. She stood up and walked over to the printer in the corner of the room. She collected the paperwork and walked back to him.

"Here you are, sir," she said. She placed the paperwork on his table.

"Why do you address me as sir?" he asked. Her eyes danced in confusion.

"How else shall I address you?"

"By my proper title, Sheikh Asaad."

"Ah. Sir just kind of rolls off the tongue." Fadi raised an eyebrow. Jane cleared her throat. "I will address you as sheikh." She grinned at him.

"Mmm-hmm."

Jane put her laptop back in her bag. "I'm going home," she said. Fadi did not say anything. He just winked at her. Jane's eyes widened. "Did you just… okay… bye," she stammered. She looked so awkward, like she did not know what to say. Fadi wanted to laugh. She was such a confident and feisty woman, but a wink made her that awkward. He watched her rush out of the room so quickly.

Chapter 9

Jane

Jane clung to her bag straps in confusion. She stood outside of Fadi's house, wondering if he had just winked at her. It was just so random. Maybe he had something in his eye, but it made her heart flutter. She groaned in frustration. She did not want to fall for him. No way. He was a rich and arrogant sheikh. They were worlds apart. He was her boss and she was his employee. There was no use in thinking of anything else. She shook her head and walked off his property.

Jane scrunched up her nose when she walked through her front door. She could smell her mother's perfume. Insolence. It was a unique smell. It wasn't a popular one. Jane took her shoes off and headed to the living room.

"Dad?" she said in shock. Her father was sitting on the sofa reading a newspaper. The grey-haired man looked up. A smile immediately appeared on his face.

"Janie," he said. She wrapped her arms around him and kissed his cheek.

"When did you get here?" More like why. She loved seeing her parents but surprise visits gave her no time to stock up her apartment with decent food. Her mother always complained about her poor eating habits.

"Not too long ago." He smiled and took her hands into his. "You've lost weight."

Jane laughed. "As if that is possible, Dad," she said. She was already slim, and she ate a lot. She doubted that she had lost any weight. Her dad laughed with her.

"Is that Jane?" a voice sounded from the kitchen.

"Yes!" Jane shouted back before she rushed to the kitchen. Her mother was in the kitchen cooking. Well, that wasn't shocking. Jane wrapped her arms around her mother's waist and rested her cheek upon her back. "Mom," she said.

"Regina tried to say the instant noodles were hers but I know that they're yours," her mother said. Jane rolled her eyes and released her mother from her embrace.

"I am fine, Mom. Thanks for asking."

Her mother turned to face her. "You must eat well," she said. Jane nodded.

"I know, Mom. When did you arrive? Why the sudden visit?"

"Can't I visit my baby?" Her mother raised an eyebrow. Jane laughed.

"I suppose you could." She opened a shopping bag that was sitting on the kitchen counter and took out an apple. She curled her upper lip and put the apple back in the bag.

"You should be eating more fruits," said her mother.

"Mmm." Jane was not a big fan of fruits. "Where is Regina?"

"She went to the bathroom right before you arrived."

"Oh." Jane left the kitchen and returned to the living room. She sat with her father and talked to him while her mother made dinner. When she was finished cooking, she called them to eat.

The four of them sat at the tiny wooden table in the kitchen. "The food looks good," Regina said to Jane's mother.

"Eat up," Jane's mother said with a smile. She turned her attention to Jane and took her hand into hers. "I am sorry that you have to work to pay your tuition," she said. Jane shook her head.

"It's fine," Jane replied. Her father looked at her with somber eyes.

"I have failed you," he said.

"No, Dad, you haven't. Please do not worry about me." She knew that her father was having a hard time since his business went bankrupt. The last thing she wanted was for him to feel guilty or worry about her.

"Is it too much? Working and studying?" her father asked. Jane shook her head.

"My job doesn't require much of me."

"At least dress better when you go out," said her mother. Jane narrowed her gaze. That was the second time she was hearing about how she was dressed.

"What is wrong with what I am wearing?" Jane asked.

"At this rate, I won't be getting a son-in-law."

"Oh God." Jane rolled her eyes.

"Leave her alone," said Jane's father.

Jane sighed. She cut into her chicken and started eating. She did not want to discuss marriage with her mother. That conversation was a few years too early. She was not looking to get married just yet.

"George, she's twenty-five years old. You and I got married when I was twenty-three," Jane's mother said to her father.

"This is a different generation," her father replied.

"I just want to focus on my studies for now," Jane replied. Regina looked amused as she ate her food.

"You too Regina," Jane's mother said to her.

"Me?" Regina asked.

"Yes. You are not getting any younger either. You need to settle down."

Jane and Regina looked at each other. Jane mouthed *ignore her.* Regina smiled in response.

"What is your boss like?" Jane's father asked. Jane almost chocked on her food. She did not want to talk about Fadi, especially since the wink.

"He's normal. Just like other employers," said Jane. "Please pass the salad."

Regina passed her the salad.

"Is he nice to you?" Jane's mother asked.

"He's okay. I don't speak to him that much."

"And his job, what does he do?"

"Oil business," Jane said quietly.

"Oil," her parents spat out in unison. Jane looked up from her plate and looked at them both.

"Yes?" she wondered why they were both shocked that her boss was in the oil industry.

"He's a sheikh too," Regina interjected. Jane's mother raised her eyebrows.

"Is that so? I guess you get paid well," said Jane's mother. Jane shrugged her shoulders in response. "Maybe you can ask him about a job," she added.

"I have a job," Jane replied.

"As an engineer."

"Mom, no. I can't do that."

"Why not? He works in the field that you are aiming to get into."

"When I start working in the oil industry, it will be because I went for an interview and got the job. I don't want to ask the sheikh for a job." It would be awkward if she did that. It was already awkward between them, now that he had winked at her. Besides, she was sure that he did not like her. They had argued at her interview. Even after she got the job, she saw no signs of him warming up to her. Well, there was him asking her to make a development plan. She still didn't know what that was about.

"You need to learn to use your contacts wisely," said her mother.

"He's not my contact. Just my employer."

"Janice, leave her alone," Jane's father said to his wife. Jane was grateful for her father coming to her aid. Her mother was like a dog with a bone. If Jane's father did not get involved in the conversation, her mother would go on and on.

Chapter 10

Fadi

Fadi was buttoning up his shirt when he felt his phone vibrating in his pocket. He fished it out and looked at the screen. It was his mother calling.

"Hello," he said as he answered his phone.

"Fadi, you finally picked up!" said his mother.

"I've been busy." That and the fact that he knew what she wanted to discuss, so he was avoiding her calls.

"You should never be too busy to speak to your mother."

"I trust that you've been well."

"No, I have not been well. How could I when I barely speak to my eldest child?"

Fadi rubbed the temples of his head. "I will make an effort to call you more often," he said to her.

"Not just me but your wife as well," she replied.

"I do not have a wife."

"You are going to get married soon enough anyway."

"Is that why you've been calling me? To talk about Faiza?"

"Fadi, you are going to marry Faiza. There is no point in continuing to be so cold towards her," said his mother. "You need to make time for her. She will be the mother of your children."

Fadi sighed. His mother was right but he just wasn't bothered about calling Faiza. There was nothing for them to speak about. He wasn't a person that liked speaking over the phone either.

"I will call her soon," said Fadi. That was all he could say.

"You will do more than that," said his mother. "She will be coming over for dinner next weekend. You should come home for that weekend."

"I have work to do."

"I don't understand why you insist on being so hands-on." She sighed with frustration. "You have people to do all the work. You only need to go and supervise once or twice a month."

Fadi narrowed his gaze. His mother just did not get it. If he stayed away from work for too long, workers would slack and standards would drop. His presence kept people on their toes.

His bedroom door flew open, and then Jane walked into the room. She had clean bedsheets in her arms. Her blue eyes fell to his bare chest. He had not finished buttoning his shirt when his mother called.

"Shall I come back later?" she mouthed. Fadi shook his head. He waved her over. She walked into the room and headed towards the bed. She started stripping the covers.

"Are you listening?" his mother called out.

"Sorry, Mother, I did not hear what you said." He had been looking at Jane and forgot that he was speaking to his mother. "I will come home next weekend," he said.

"Oh you will? That is wonderful. I will be delighted to see you."

"I have other matters to attend to. I shall speak to you another time." Fadi hung up and buttoned up his shirt. Jane put the dirty bedsheets in a laundry basket.

"That was your mother?" she asked. Fadi looked at her with a blank facial expression. Did she really expect him to tell her about his phone call? "That was such a cold ending to the call. You did not even say goodbye or take care."

"I always speak to her like that," he replied.

"That doesn't make it any better." She put a clean cream-colored sheet on the bed. "You need to speak to her more lovingly."

"I thought that was fine." He suddenly felt defensive. Jane shook her head in disagreement.

"Does she call you all the time?"

"I always have a missed call from her every other day."

Jane laughed a little. "I bet she nags you about not calling or visiting," she said.

"Precisely," he replied.

"My mother is like that." Jane started changing the pillowcases. "I think all mothers are like that. You just have to be extra sweet when you do speak to her."

"Is that what you do?" Fadi asked. He was suddenly curious about her life.

"No." Jane laughed. "I'm not a sweet person but I am definitely much warmer than you." Her eyes flew wide open. She cleared her throat and looked down.

"Don't start feeling bad about speaking so informally to me. You have been doing it for a while," he said sarcastically. Jane put her hand over her mouth and laughed guiltily.

"I am so sorry. I know I need to work on that. My mother always tells me that I have an impulsive tongue," she said and bowed her head. She never bowed her head to him.

"Your mother's words are accurate," said Fadi. Jane smiled and spread the covers onto the bed. As she was walking to the other side of the bed, she kicked the bed.

"Argh!" she cried out. She immediately grabbed her foot in her hands and started jumping around on the other foot. Fadi smiled as he watched her clumsiness. She was quite clumsy. It was both amusing and adorable at the same time.

"Why are you this clumsy?" he asked her.

"It hurts." Her voice squeaked.

"You'll live."

Jane let go of her foot and stood properly on two feet. "That hurt my small toe," she complained.

"You need to be more careful." Fadi headed for the door. He paused in the doorway and looked at Jane. "I am going out for dinner," he said. Jane opened her mouth and closed it.

"That is fine, sir," she said. "Sheikh Asaad," she corrected herself. He could tell that she wanted to complain but held back.

"It's not like you had started cooking," he said to her.

"I had thawed and marinated the meat. The rice is in the rice cooker too," she mumbled. "But it's fine." She forced a grin. She was so animated. It was amusing to watch. Fadi smiled to himself as he walked out of the room.

***

Jane

Jane wanted to throw a shoe at Fadi's head as he walked out of the bedroom. She had already made the preparations for dinner. It would have saved her a lot of time and effort if he had told her that he was going out for dinner an hour or two earlier. Jane sighed. She kept on with the bedding.

For the first time, Jane and Fadi had had a normal conversation. Sort of. They had spoken about their mothers. She was curious to learn about him. He was a peculiar man. She had unintentionally spoken informally to him but he had not fired her or yelled at her. She did not understand why he was keeping her on. Why did he hire her in the first place?

After Jane finished changing the bedding, she cleaned Fadi's enormous bedroom. Not that it was dirty in the first place. Everything was so clean and tidy. Fadi was such a neat man. However, there was no warmth in his bedroom. Jane noticed that there were no pictures of his family on the wall or on the nightstand. There were no signs of another woman's presence. The bedroom looked like a hotel bedroom. There was nothing homey about it.

Maybe Fadi was a lonely man. It probably was not easy to be a sheikh. People would want to be around him to further their careers and social status. Women would want money and luxuries from him. Maybe that could explain his cold personality. She suddenly felt sorry for him.

Jane took the dirty sheets and the clothes that needed to be washed out of Fadi's bedroom. She winced when she felt a slight pain in her left small toe. She had stubbed it when she kicked the bed. It was embarrassing how she had managed to do that in Fadi's presence. That bastard, Jane thought to herself. He had said to her *you won't die*. He didn't even ask her if she was okay. That handsome bastard. Jane had caught a glimpse of his bare chest when she had walked in. The image was burned in her brain. She was never going to forget it.

Chapter 11

Jane

"Follow me," Fadi said to Jane as she walked through the front door. Jane watched him walk past her and out the front door. A thousand thoughts rushed through her mind. Where was he taking her? Was he going to fire her? Had she not done something correctly?

"Where are we going?" Jane asked as Fadi headed towards the white Bentley parked in front of the house. He opened the backseat door.

"Get in," he said to her. Jane stared at him in confusion.

"Um, sir?"

"We are going somewhere. Get in."

Jane hesitated for a moment. Then she climbed into the backseat of the car that was worth more than her apartment. She wasn't surprised when she saw that the car seats were white. Fadi was slightly obsessed with the damn color. Jane placed her bag by her feet. She was still in her leggings and sweater. She hadn't changed into her uniform yet.

The driver was already in the car. Fadi got in and sat next to Jane in the backseat. "Let's go," he said to the driver. Fadi shut the door and buckled his seatbelt. Jane instantly did the same. They drove off Fadi's estate.

"Sheikh Asaad," Jane called. Fadi raised an eyebrow and looked at her.

"Sheikh Asaad?" he asked. He looked amused. Jane narrowed her gaze. Why was he amused that she had called him by his proper title? He had asked her to do so instead of calling him sir.

"Where are we going?" she asked.

"Asaad Refinery," he said. Jane blinked a few times and waited for him to elaborate. "My oil refinery," he added. Jane gasped louder than she wanted.

"You have oil refineries too?"

"Just this one. I wanted to expand our family business further."

"That's amazing, but it must have cost you a lot to start refining oil. A lot of equipment and experienced engineers are needed."

Fadi nodded. "Price doesn't matter, as long as the quality is high," he said. Price always mattered, Jane thought to herself. She had never been that close to Fadi. It wasn't easy being that close to such an attractive man. On top of that, he smelled so good.

"So your family company normally just drills for oil and sells it?" Jane asked Fadi. She had to talk, to do something to stop herself from noticing his sexiness and thinking about it. He shot her a quick glance.

"You work for me and yet you know nothing about me," he said. Jane laughed guiltily.

"Well, I work as your maid. Therefore, I need to know what you like to eat and how you want your bed made," said Jane. Fadi looked at her with a mischievous grin on his face. She gave him a questioning glare.

"To you, it is only important to know about my bed?"

Jane's jaw dropped open. That wasn't even close to what she had meant. A loose tendril tumbled down her forehead. Fadi reached out and moved it off her face. Jane's eyes slowly widened. Fadi was unpredictable and full of surprises. What was he touching her hair for? It was already hard enough being so close to him, and now he was touching her hair. Torture.

"We only sell oil but I wanted to get into the refinery business. I have been interested in it," he said. Jane sighed with relief. She preferred talking about refining oil rather than his bed.

"That's why you work a lot, because you are still getting the refinery up and running," she said. Fadi answered her with a grunt.

The ride to the refinery was forty minutes long. The refinery was located on the outskirts of Boston. She was grateful when they arrived. She hated long journeys. She jumped of the car and stretched her muscles.

Jane had been to a refinery in Washington once on a university trip. She was glad to have the opportunity to visit one again. She had no idea why Fadi had invited her but she was glad. She followed him towards the engineers that were waiting for him. They greeted him with a bow when he approached. A tall man with jet-black hair and hazel eyes approached Jane and Fadi. He shook Fadi's hand and spoke in Arabic. It was the first time Jane had heard Fadi speaking in Arabic. It was really quite alluring.

"Who is she?" the man asked Fadi as he nodded in Jane's direction.

"Jane," he replied. The man raised his eyebrows in confusion. He looked at Jane and then back at Fadi. He asked Fadi something in Arabic. Fadi narrowed his gaze at him before he replied. Jane wondered just what they were talking about.

"Hello Jane. My name is Sofian." He offered his hand to her. Jane smiled before she shook it.

"Hi Sofian," said Jane. Sofian was about two inches shorter than Fadi. His body was not as muscular but it was still quite impressive. Sofian offered Jane a yellow helmet. She took the helmet and put it on. Sofian and Fadi also put on helmets.

Sofian gave Fadi and Jane a tour of the refinery. There were large metal pipes all around. The machinery was already set up but there was still some equipment lying about. Jane could tell that they were still building the refinery. Despite the warning to be careful, Jane tripped over a copper pipe. She went stumbling forward with a loud squeak. Fadi grabbed her arm and stopped her from falling over.

Fadi looked at her and grunted. Jane glared at the pipe as if the pipe had crawled into her way, when it was her fault for being clumsy. "Here," Fadi gave Jane his elbow. Sofian raised his eyebrows and slid his hands into his pockets. He stared at Jane with a mischievous grin on his face as he waited for her response.

"You want me to hold your arm?" Jane asked. "I'll be fine." She felt awkward about holding his arm, and Sofian's expression made her feel shy.

"No you won't. Just take it before you hurt yourself."

Fadi had a point. Jane would probably fall over again at some point. An oil refinery under construction was the wrong place to be so clumsy. She could possibly fall on a piece of metal and break her leg. It would be painful and embarrassing. Jane slowly held onto

Fadi's muscular arm. She felt awkward about doing so.

Jane quickly settled into Fadi's warmth. She felt so comfortable and at ease as they toured the refinery. It wasn't a grand refinery like the one she had seen in Washington but it was large enough to refine large quantities of crude oil.

"When will everything be finished?" Fadi asked Sofian.

"In a week," he replied. Fadi nodded. "It was nice to meet you, Jane," he said with a smile.

"It was nice to meet you too. Thank you for the tour." Jane nodded. Sofian tipped his helmet to her like a cowboy before he walked off.

Fadi and Jane headed back to the car. The driver was waiting for them outside the car. He opened the backseat door for them. They both climbed into the backseat as Fadi checked the expensive Rolex sitting on his wrist.

"Take us to the nearest restaurant," he said to his driver.

"Yes sheikh," the driver replied before starting the car engine.

"We are going to a restaurant now?" Jane asked Fadi. "Are you meeting someone?"

"You ask a lot of questions."

"Sir, you do not share enough information." It was only natural that she was curious. Fadi had a habit of just telling her what to do without explanation.

"I am hungry," he said as they drove off. Jane suddenly realized that she was hungry also. It had been three hours since she had eaten, and for her that was a very long time.

Fadi led Jane into a quaint little restaurant. There weren't many people in there. A blond waitress greeted them and showed them to an empty table. She provided them both with menus. Jane watched Fadi read his menu. He was acting so normal as if they had been to a restaurant together before. First he had offered her his arm and now he had taken her to a restaurant. She felt a little awkward about everything. Just a little bit.

"What will you be having?" Fadi asked Jane. She quickly looked down at her menu.

"I think steak and fries," she said.

"Mmm. I do not see any other options. I guess it will have to be some unhealthy fries." He frowned. He closed his menu and placed it on the table. Jane smiled. He was so picky.

The waitress came to get their orders. Her attention was rather fixed on Fadi. She listened to him with a smile as he spoke but when Jane spoke, she barely looked at her. "I'll bring your order as soon as it's ready," she said in the smallest voice ever with her head tilted to the side. It was not cute. It was just weird. Jane could not help but roll her eyes.

I'll bring your order as soon as it's ready. Really? We thought that you would bring it after 24 hours, said Jane's subconscious sardonically.

Chapter 12

Fadi

Fadi and Jane waited for their food in silence. She sat across from him dressed messily. This time he was not surprised. Very little about her surprised him now. He was starting to get used to her little traits and mannerisms. He wasn't surprised when she had nearly fallen over at the refinery. She was a very clumsy girl. It was amusing. Jane turned her head to face Fadi and found him already staring at her. She widened her eyes.

"Sir?" she asked.

"You are an odd woman," he said.

"Then why did you bring me here with you? Surely you do not want to spend your Sunday afternoon with an odd woman."

Her alto voice was attractive. It oozed with confidence. Normally a deeper voice on a woman exuded sex appeal but it was not the case with Jane. She probably knew nothing about sex appeal and interaction with the opposite sex. Fadi could just tell, and his suspicions were confirmed when he mentioned his bed. She was so shocked and did not know what to say. She was more confident about a lot of things but not men. Fadi had seen how she froze when he touched her hair.

"I thought you would be interested in seeing my refinery," he said. "What did you think about it?"

"It's coming along nicely. Is it just to refine your oil or are you open to refining oil for other companies?" she said.

"Just our oil at first, then we will reach out to others."

The waitress appeared with their lunch. She served Fadi first. As she should. He was the sheikh after all. She served him with a big smile. Fadi noticed that her top button had been unbuttoned. She gave Jane her lunch and then returned her attention to Fadi.

"Is there anything else that I could get you, sir?" she asked.

"No," Fadi replied.

"I would like–" Jane began to say but the waitress cut her off.

"Please call me if you need anything." She winked at Fadi before she left. Jane burst into laughter.

"Wow, the nerve of her," said Jane.

"What is the matter?" Fadi picked up his fork and knife.

"She was shamelessly flirting with you and ignoring me as if I wasn't here. What if I was your wife?"

"You want to be my woman?" he asked. Jane looked up from her plate so fast he was surprised that she did not get whiplash.

"What? That's not what I said. Why would you ask me that?" She blushed. Interesting. Why did she get that shy?

"You are annoyed about her flirting with me, and you did not answer my question."

"I am annoyed by her unprofessional slutty behavior. She completely ignored me when I was about to ask for pepper. And no, I don't want to be your woman." She cut into her steak and ate a piece. Fadi smiled before he started eating also.

There was silence between them for a minute. Fadi had only eaten two mouthfuls of food when he caught Jane frowning. She jerked her head forward and looked at Fadi. She looked down and cut a piece of her steak.

"Say whatever it is that you want to say," he said to her.

"I have nothing to say," she replied. Fadi looked at her with a blank facial expression. She never held back her thoughts, so why now? "This steak doesn't taste good," she said. Fadi put his fork and knife on the plate.

"It tastes horrible," he replied. Maybe it was because Fadi was used to Jane's cooking but Fadi found the restaurant's food disgusting. Jane burst into laughter. Fadi called over the waitress.

"You called me over quickly. What can I get you, sir?" she asked.

"The bill," Fadi replied.

"You don't have to pay until you have finished eating."

"We are finished."

The waitress looked at him in confusion before she went to retrieve the bill. Fadi quickly paid for the food. "Let's go," he said to Jane.

"We can't just leave all this food," she said to him.

"We can and we will." Fadi rose from his seat. Jane stood up and quickly followed him out of the restaurant.

"Your girlfriend in there must be disappointed. You did not finish your food nor did you tip her," said Jane. Fadi slipped his hands in his pockets and looked at Jane as they walked back to the car.

"My girlfriend," he repeated.

"I noticed how she unbuttoned her top for you."

"You are just jealous because she is more endowed than you."

Jane burst into laughter. "I have never been bothered by my small chest," she replied. Fadi raised his eyebrows. Most women he knew would have wanted breast augmentation. He was pleasantly surprised that Jane was comfortable and confident with her size.

"Mmm-hmm."

They reached Fadi's car. The driver opened the door for them. They climbed into the car. The aftertaste of the food was so bad, Fadi had lost his appetite.

"I have never tasted food so disgusting," said Jane.

"That restaurant ought to be closed down," Fadi replied. "Do you want to go anywhere else?"

"Let's go home. I will cook."

"Home."

"Your home," Jane spat out. "Today, everything I say seems to have an alternative meaning apparently."

Fadi smirked. It was quite amusing to play with her words. He knew what she meant but it was funny how she reacted when he pretended not to know what she meant. Her reactions were so animated.

The ride back to his home was almost an hour long. When they arrived back at his estate, Fadi went upstairs to change. Jane went to the kitchen to prepare food for him. He was relieved when the food was ready. He couldn't believe himself but he had actually missed her food.

Chapter 13

Jane

On Thursday night, Jane met up with some of her classmates. They had a group presentation to prepare for. Jane wasn't so keen on presentations. She was not shy but she did not like the hassle of presenting.

"We have to do really well on this presentation. I want to work for the Asaad oil company when I graduate," said Mark, one of Jane's classmates. Jane whipped her head in his direction when she heard Fadi's surname.

"You have to graduate with a GPA more than 3.9 to work there," Jason replied. Jane leaned back in her chair.

"That is a little bit too high," said Jane.

"Fadi Asaad only hires the best of the best."

"3.9 is quite high though."

"My overall grade point comes to 3.7 at the moment. I need to do better on this presentation and all future assignments," said Mark.

"Fadi is handsome. I would not mind working for him," said Stacey, a blond with a high-pitched voice and the only other girl in Jane's presentation group. There were five guys and two girls.

"You better get a good grade then," said Mark.

"There is no chance of that happening," Peter joked. Stacey frowned.

"That is not funny," she complained.

Jane sat there quietly. She felt like gloating a little bit. She had worked on a development plan with Fadi and she had been to his refinery. She got to see him every weekend. She smiled to herself when she remembered the feeling of his hard and warm arm. Jane couldn't figure him out. He was cold but then he was nice to her in an odd way. When she had nearly fallen over, he did not ask if she was okay but he gave her his arm.

Fadi had asked her if she wanted to be his woman. Jane could still remember how she had felt hearing those words. Her insides had melted like butter in a hot pan. He had looked at her so seriously as if he was really asking her, but Jane knew better. She couldn't imagine what life would be like as his woman. He would probably not show her affection. He couldn't even be warm to his own mother, much less a mere woman. Kissing him, though, that would...

"Jane!" Stacey called out and interrupted her thoughts. Jane snapped out of her thoughts and looked at the annoying blond. "I've been speaking to you."

"Sorry, what did you say?" Jane had gotten so lost in her thoughts. Thoughts of Fadi had completely taken over her mind.

"Have you completed your section of the presentation?" Stacey flipped her hair. That was about the tenth time she had done so within the last five minutes.

"Yeah." Jane opened her bag and pulled out her notes. She showed them and explained what she had done.

***

Jane showed up at work on time the next day. She changed into her uniform as she usually did. She met Mariam on her way out of the bathroom. That was the first time she had seen her since she stormed out of Fadi's office.

"Hi Mariam," said Jane.

"The sheikh is looking for you," she said.

"Where is he?"

"In his bedroom."

Jane nodded before she walked off. She headed up the stairs and then down the hallway. She knocked on Fadi's bedroom door.

"Come in," he called out. Jane slid the doors open and walked in. Fadi was standing over an open suitcase. Jane raised her eyebrows.

"Going somewhere?" she asked as she approached him.

"Al Hamri," he replied.

"Oh that's nice. For how long?"

"Just the weekend."

That meant she was not going to see him for a full week. That did not quite sit well with Jane. She had gotten so used to seeing him every weekend. She wanted to slap herself for her mixed feelings.

"Why do you look like you are about to cry?" Fadi asked Jane.

"What?" Jane frowned. "Why would I want to cry?"

Fadi slipped his hands in his pockets and looked down at Jane. Even though she was taller than the average woman, she was much shorter than Fadi. His height made him even more attractive.

"Your face changed when I told you that I would be gone for the weekend," he said. Suddenly his voice had gone deeper. It made Jane's knees buckle. She forced a smile.

"I will be able to clean in peace." She did not even know what she meant by that. He never bothered her when she cleaned. She just needed to say something to make him think that she was unbothered by his absence.

Fadi raised his eyebrows and smiled a little. Even though he did not believe her. "You don't have to clean," he said.

"Why don't I?"

"I have something else for you."

Fadi adjusted his belt buckle. Jane's eyes flew wide open. She leaped backwards. "What do you have for me?" she shouted. Fadi looked at her as though she had gone mad.

"My belt is a little uncomfortable. I was just shifting it into a more comfortable place," he said before bursting into laughter. That was the first time she had seen him laughing so hard and it was at her expense.

"The timing was rather off," Jane admitted. She touched her red cheeks. She felt slightly embarrassed.

"What kind of strange thoughts do you have in your head?"

"Nothing strange." She wanted the ground to just open up and swallow her. Fadi turned his head and walked over to the nightstand. He picked up two blue folders and re-approached Jane. He handed her the folders.

"What is this?" Jane asked as she accepted the folders.

"I need another development plan for a different oil well," he said. Jane raised her eyebrows. He was entrusting her with another task? Excitement crept through her. "I also need you to interpret these well-logging results and produce a short report on that reservoir," he added.

More work! Jane couldn't hide her smile. "You're giving me more work?" she asked.

"Take the weekend off and do that instead," he said.

"But don't you have far more experienced people to do this for you?"

"I want you to do it."

Jane smiled. Whatever his reason was, she was happy to do it. "Okay," she replied. She clutched the folders tightly. "Do you want to eat before you leave?" she asked him.

"No."

"How long is your flight?"

"Twelve hours."

Jane raised her eyebrows. "That is a long journey," she said. She would hate to sit for that long. "Are you going for business or pleasure?" she asked. Fadi had no expression on his face.

"You ask a lot of questions," he said. Jane opened her mouth slightly and then closed it. She really did ask a lot of questions.

"Have a safe flight, sir," she said. As she turned on her heel, she stepped on the suitcase handle and lost her balance. Damn, she cursed silently. She was going to fall over in front of Fadi again. Before she knew it, his arm was snaked around her waist. He pulled her closer to him and her back slammed into his chest.

"Why are you so clumsy?" he growled. Jane's heart raced inside her chest. She could feel Fadi's rock-hard chest. She had been close to him before but not that close. She wanted to flee from him but her legs froze.

"Are you planning to stay in my arms forever?" Fadi whispered in Jane's ear.

"Um… thanks for catching me." She turned around to face him. Her eyes met his. Before she could think or do anything, Fadi pulled her close to her and held her tightly. He stared deeply into her eyes as he moved his face closer to hers. He pressed his lips against hers. Jane inhaled sharply.

"What are you doing?" she whispered. As if it was not obvious. Fadi responded by gently pushing his tongue into her mouth. He slowly kissed her as though she was delicate. His lips were soft and delicious. Jane thought she was going to shatter into a thousand pieces. She had only been kissed by one other man and there had been no involvement of tongues.

Fadi held her body tightly and slowly caressed her back as he kissed her. She stood there awkwardly with her arms dangling at her sides. Fadi broke off the kiss. Jane stood there with her eyes closed.

"Feel free to open your eyes," he teased. Jane opened her eyes and cleared her throat. She touched the back of her neck. She wanted him to kiss her again.

"That... was..." Jane struggled to find her words. "Unexpected," she finished off. Fadi picked up his suitcase.

"I have to go now," he said. He headed for the door and left Jane standing in the middle of his bedroom full of mixed feelings. She was so turned on by Fadi's passionate kiss but confused as to why he did it and angry because he stopped and then left her.

Chapter 14

Fadi

By the time Fadi arrived at his family estate in Al Hamri, it was 9 a.m. He was greeted at the door by Maria. She was the head maid of the house. He had known her his entire life. She had always looked after him growing up and so he was close to her. She was like an aunt.

"How was your flight?" she asked.

"It was fine," he replied. She rubbed his arm and smiled.

"Your parents are in the dining room."

Fadi nodded before he made his way to the dining room.

"My son," his mother breathed as she rose to her feet.

"Mother." Fadi kissed her on both cheeks.

"Good to have you back, son." Sheikh Asaad Senior, Fadi's father, extended his hand for a handshake. Fadi shook his father's hand. That was normal for them. They did not hug or kiss. A handshake was about as much affection as they could share.

"It's good to be back," Fadi replied as he pulled up a seat for himself at the table. A maid immediately approached with a plate and cutlery.

"I am so happy that you came," said his mother.

"You look well."

"I cannot complain."

"How is business?" Sheikh Asaad Senior asked his son.

"I have finally built the refinery," Fadi replied. Fadi wasn't a talker. He only told his father about the refinery once before. He never updated his father on everything he did in regards to business. His father let him control all their business located in America. Fadi was going to be the heir of the company anyway. Therefore, his father handed him the reins quite early on.

"How much did it cost?" Sheikh Asaad Senior asked.

"$250 million," Fadi replied. His mother gasped.

"Isn't that expensive?" she asked.

"No. Oil refineries are usually more expensive," her husband replied.

"Then why was yours so cheap?" his mother asked. She did not know much about the oil and gas business. After she married Sheikh Asaad Senior, she focused on running the home and raising the children.

"It's a small one," said Fadi. Since it was his first, he wanted to start small. Eventually he would expand.

"I suspect that you did not use any investors," said Fadi's father. Fadi was never fond of investors because he preferred to have full controlling power.

"No," Fadi replied.

"Is that wise?" his mother asked.

"No, it's not. If the refinery fails, he will lose all his money," said Sheikh Asaad senior.

"It won't fail," Fadi replied. His father smiled and shook his head.

"My son is very hardheaded. I hope you can break even at least."

"I will profit."

"He gets that overconfidence from you," his mother said to his father. Fadi and his father both smiled because she was right.

"Faiza will be glad to see you tomorrow," Fadi's mother said with a big smile on her face. She was the only one excited about the marriage. Fadi's father was indifferent. She thought Faiza was a beautiful woman from an esteemed family; which was true. However, she was also in a rush for Fadi to have children. She really wanted to be a grandmother.

"I am going upstairs," said Fadi as he took a sip of his tea. He really did not know what to say to his mother.

"Why do you never have anything to say when it comes to Faiza? She is going to be your wife, Fadi. You need to warm up to her sooner or later," said his mother. She looked so frustrated with her son. Her husband raised his eyebrows and sighed.

"Stop frustrating your mother," he said. "Just call the girl once or twice, and smile at her when you see her," he added. Fadi shrugged his shoulders.

"I will be kind to her tomorrow," he said as he rose to his feet. He left the room and headed up to his bedroom. The flight from Boston to Al Hamri had been so long. He just wanted to rest.

Fadi was almost falling asleep when he heard an annoying and familiar voice. "Fadi!" the voice screeched out before Fadi felt someone jumping on his bed.

"Amina." Fadi groaned. Amina was Fadi's little sister. She was the youngest in the family. Fadi was the eldest followed by his younger brother Beshoy and then Amina.

"Why are you sleeping without looking for me?" Amina complained.

"I'm tired."

"Fadi!" Amina tugged on his arm. "Didn't you miss me?"

"There was no one to disturb my sleep," he said.

"Fadi!" Amina cried out. He rolled his head to the side and looked at her.

"You changed your hair color again," he said as he looked at her burgundy hair.

"Mum does not like it," Amina giggled.

"Of course she doesn't." Fadi could just picture how angry his mother was when she saw Amina's hair. Their mother wanted Amina to look like a typical Arabic girl from a respectable family. However, Amina had ideas of her own. She was always up to something her parents did not approve of. "I brought you something," he said to her.

"What?" Amina's face lit up.

"Check my jacket." Fadi pointed at the leather club chair opposite his bed. Amina jumped off his bed and rushed over. She searched the jacket until she found a velvet box. She opened it and screamed when she saw the contents.

"These are the diamond earrings I wanted!" Amina rushed to Fadi's side and kissed him on the cheek. "Thank you." She giggled.

"Now leave me," said Fadi. He rolled his head and faced the other side.

"Okay, have a good rest." Amina slammed the door on her way out. Fadi groaned. She was always so noisy.

***

Fadi slipped into a pair of black cherry trousers and a navy-blue polo shirt. He wore a pair of navy-blue loafers. He left his bedroom and headed downstairs to join his family in the courtyard.

"You look dashing," Amina complimented Fadi as he walked outside. She and the rest of his family were already sitting at the marble table in the middle of the courtyard.

"As do you," Fadi replied. Amina had her burgundy hair tied up into a high ponytail. She wore a navy-blue boatneck skater dress and a pair of black pointy-toe high heels.

"Just three months left of your freedom," Beshoy teased Fadi as he approached him. Beshoy wore a pair of khaki trousers and a polo shirt.

"Those three months couldn't come sooner," said their mother. She was elegantly dressed as usual. She wore a long-sleeved green dress and white pearls. Her hair was neatly pinned up. Her husband wore a traditional outfit of loose-fitting black slacks and a white knee-length shirt.

A maid walked out onto the courtyard with Faiza and her mother, the queen. They were accompanied by a few bodyguards. Faiza wore a boatneck white dress with lace sleeves and a ruby necklace worth thousands of dollars. Her jet-black hair was tied up. Her mother wore a royal-blue long-sleeved dress with silver embroidery. Her dark brown hair was pinned up neatly.

Fadi and his family all bowed their heads as Faiza and her mother approached them. Fadi's mother and the queen greeted each other warmly. Faiza and Fadi made eye contact. Fadi gave her a small bow. She smiled in response. They all sat down at the marble table.

"Fadi has grown into a handsome young man," said the queen. Even though Fadi and Faiza were betrothed, they barely saw each other. Fadi was always in Boston working, and the palace was not a place people could come and go as they pleased. Faiza was usually busy with a charity event or royal parties.

"I cannot take credit for that," said Lady Asaad, Fadi's mother. "He takes after his father," she added with a smile.

"He is the spitting image of his father indeed," the queen replied. "How is business in Boston?" she asked Fadi.

"Business is good," he replied. The maids walked out onto the courtyard with trays of traditional Arabic foods. They set them on the table and then served everyone.

Faiza sat opposite Fadi. She stole glances at him every moment she could. Fadi had noticed but he was unbothered. As they ate their lunch, the queen and Lady Asaad did most of the talking. Sheikh Asaad Senior uttered a few words.

"Fadi and the princess should go for a walk," Lady Asaad suggested when they were finished eating lunch.

"That is a lovely idea. The couple should get some alone time," said the queen. Fadi watched Faiza's face light up. Clearly she was pleased with the idea.

Chapter 15

Fadi

Fadi rose to his feet and walked around the table to Faiza. He offered her his palm. She placed her palm into his and then he helped her up to her feet. The two of them headed off for their walk.

"It has been a while since we've met," Faiza said to Fadi.

"It has indeed," he replied. Even though they had met before, they had never been alone. There was always someone present. Now that they were alone, it was rather awkward. Fadi did not know what to say to her.

"What is it like in Boston? I have been to New York and Los Angeles but not Boston," said Faiza. Clearly she did not know what to say either.

"It's fine. It gets cold. Winter should be starting soon."

"Do you wish for us to live there when we are married?"

Fadi raised an eyebrow. He hadn't even given it a thought. It was a good question though. Where were they going to live when they were married? He liked being able to travel between Al Hamri and Boston.

However, he could not imagine having Faiza in Boston with him.

"Where would you like to live?" Fadi asked her.

"I am used to living in Al Hamri but I don't mind a change." Faiza looked at Fadi and smiled. "Wherever you want to go, I am fine with it."

Fadi just nodded. They walked onto the green grass. Miles of green grass stretched out before them. It was the perfect place for a walk. Fadi would probably have enjoyed the walk more if it was just him alone.

If Fadi was with Jane, there would have been more conversation. Jane always had something to say. She was talkative and funny. Speaking of Jane, the last time he had seen her, they were in his bedroom kissing. It wasn't something he had planned but the moment her body was against his, he knew that he had to kiss her. Fadi could still remember how soft and sweet her lips tasted.

"Fadi," Faiza said softly.

"Yes," Fadi replied.

"My father would like to meet you soon. He was unable to come today because he always has so much work to do. But, he will invite you to the palace."

"I will be happy to oblige."

"Great. You and my father need to meet. After all, our wedding is only three months away."

Three months too soon.

After their walk, Fadi and Faiza returned to the courtyard. Amina stared at Fadi with a mischievous glare. Fadi narrowed his gaze at her.

"Did you have a good walk?" the queen asked Fadi and Faiza.

"Yes we did," Faiza replied with a smile.

Faiza and Fadi rejoined everyone at the table. Fadi sat between Amina and Beshoy. The maids served some tea in glass cups.

"They were already talking about the wedding," Amina whispered to Fadi.

"Faiza is beautiful. Why are you not warming up to her?" Beshoy whispered to Fadi.

Fadi sighed. He already regretted sitting between his siblings. He knew that they were going to keep talking to him about it. He picked up his cup of tea and took a sip.

"Am I going to be a bridesmaid?" Amina whispered to Fadi. He looked at her with a raised eyebrow.

"I will be the best man," said Beshoy with a wink.

"Both of you, stop talking to me." Fadi was always the serious one. Beshoy and Amina were always joking and trying to get on his nerves.

"I can't wait to be an aunt," said Amina.

"And I an uncle," Beshoy added.

"What are the three of you whispering about over there?" Lady Asaad asked her children.

"Nothing of importance," said Fadi. Amina giggled.

Faiza and her mother stayed for a little while longer. Fadi felt relieved when they left. The visit had dragged on for longer than needed. He wondered what his marital life with Faiza would be like. Would he just get on with it or would it be really terrible?

***

Jane

Jane was sitting on the sofa with her paperwork. She was working on the assignment Fadi had left for her. Regina walked into the living room wearing a strapless red dress. Her curves looked delicious. She had silk-pressed her afro hair. The hair lay beautifully on her shoulders.

"You look nice," Jane said to Regina. Jane was wearing a loose-fitting grey tracksuit and a grey hoody. Her hair was tied up in a messy bun and she was wearing her oversized glasses for close work.

"Thank you. I hope Jason thinks so," Regina replied. She had been in a relationship with Jason for two years. Jason loved Regina so much, it was obvious.

Jane had only ever been on half a date. It had been a blind date. The guy left after she tripped and spilled her drink on him.

"Oh, Gina. Of course, Jason will love your outfit," said Jane. The doorbell rang.

"That's him." Regina dashed out of the living room. Jane heard Regina open the door and exchange pleasantries with Jason.

"Hey Jane!" Jason called out.

"Hey Jason!" Jane shouted back.

"Do you want to come with us for dinner?"

"No! I have work to do. Have fun."

"Okay, bye!" he shouted. Jane sighed when she heard the front door slam. Jason was always so considerate towards her. However, Jane was not going to be a third wheel on their date. It was not easy being the single friend.

She looked at the development plan she had been working on. It reminded her of Fadi. She had been trying so hard not to fall for him but she had failed miserably. He had made it worse when he had kissed her. She did not know why he had kissed her. She was bad at decoding men. She did not understand why they did what they did. She couldn't read signs.

Jane really did not understand Fadi. She had thought he hated her or disliked her but he was giving her these development plans to work on. He had shown her his refinery and then kissed her before he left for Al Hamri. It was Jane's first real kiss. A boy had pecked her on the lips when she was younger. He had only done so because of a dare.

The kiss Jane had shared with Fadi was every bit of amazing. He only kissed her lips but she felt the pleasure all over her body. She did not know that a kiss could do that. Jane wondered if Fadi had enjoyed it. He probably did not. Jane did not know anything about kissing. She did not even know what she had done with her tongue. She did not know if she responded or not. Her arms had just dangled awkwardly at her sides.

Oh God, Fadi smelled so nice and his body felt so good against Jane's. His body was hard. It was as if it had been carved out of stone. Jane regretted not touching his chest or even his biceps. Who knew when that chance was going arise again? Probably never.

Chapter 16

Jane

Jane boiled some water and steamed her face for a couple of minutes. Then she mixed some avocado, honey and plain yogurt and applied it on her face for twenty minutes. She washed her face and then her body. She slipped into blue jeans, a white T-shirt and a black leather jacket. She straightened her wavy hair with a styling iron and then tied it up.

She wanted to look her best. She was going to be facing Fadi after a week of separation. The last time she had seen him, they were kissing in the middle of his bedroom. She did not know what it was going to be like seeing him again. Was he going to kiss her again or was he going to wonder why he did so in the first place and just pretend it never happened? Jane was nervous.

Jane stood in the kitchen doorway. "I'm leaving for work," she said to Regina. Her friend looked up from the chopping board.

"The sheikh is back in town," Regina said with a smile.

"Yeah, he is." Jane's voice was unusually high. Regina raised an eyebrow.

"Jane?"

"Bye."

"No. Jane, what are you hiding?" Regina put the knife down and walked towards the door. Jane hadn't told her about the kiss.

"Nothing at all. Today is just the day I show him the development plan. I'm just a bit worried." Jane headed to the front door.

"Whatever!" Regina called out after her.

Jane arrived at Fadi's house right on time. She changed into her uniform and then headed to the kitchen and started cooking. It felt endless. She just wanted to see Fadi already yet part of her did not want to. The inevitable rejection scared her. She had to hurry up and face the awkward situation awaiting her.

When she finished cooking, Jane went to set the dining table. She nearly jumped out of her skin when she saw Fadi sitting at the table with a tablet. Usually he was in his office and she would have to go and call him. "Shit," Jane whispered. Fadi looked up from his tablet.

"Jane?" Fadi said.

"I didn't expect you to be here."

"In my house?"

"In the dining room. Normally you're in the office." Jane walked over to the table and placed the plate on the table. Fadi put the tablet down. His eyes rested on Jane. He watched her putting the cutlery on the table, then walking out of the room and coming back with the food. He always watched her but this time was very awkward. More awkward than usual.

"I finished working on the development plan and the well-logging results," Jane said.

"Show me," Fadi said as he picked up his fork.

"Okay." Jane walked out of the dining room and went to retrieve the documents. When she returned to the dining room, she put the folders on the table.

Jane stood by the door as usual and waited while Fadi ate and looked through the folders. Silence stretched between them as Fadi looked through the paperwork. He looked so gorgeous when he focused on something. She liked how his jaw clenched.

"You did a good job," he said.

"Thank you," Jane replied. She laced her fingers together as she wondered what to say or do next. "How was your trip?" she asked.

"Fine." One-word answer. Jane was disappointed. Even though she and Fadi did not talk much, she hoped for more conversation. Or maybe she expected him to tell her that he was thinking about her and then kiss her again.

When Fadi was finished eating, he left the dining room. Jane cleared the table and took the dishes back to the kitchen. She washed them and cleaned up. She had expected Fadi to act as though nothing had happened between them but she felt bad. She had even used a face mask and straightened her hair. Her efforts were fruitless.

"Jane," Fadi sounded from behind Jane just as she was getting ready to leave. She turned around to face the handsome man standing in the doorway. She wanted to leap into his muscular arms and slap him at the same time.

"Yes sir," she replied.

"Tomorrow, come in at 2 but don't bring your uniform."

"Um, okay?" Jane was confused but she figured Fadi was not going to share his reasons.

Fadi turned on his heel. "You straightened your hair," he said as he walked away.

"Ah, yeah." Jane wasn't sure if he liked it or not.

***

Jane arrived at Fadi's house dressed in a pair of jeans and a hoody. It was starting to get colder in Boston. Fadi was leaning against his car in the driveway waiting for her. She felt a little bit on edge. She did not know what was happening, why he had told her not to bring her uniform.

"Good afternoon," Jane greeted Fadi as she approached him.

"Jane," he said. He stood up straight. "Get in." He walked over to the driver's side. Jane raised her eyebrows.

"You're driving?" she asked him as she headed over to the passenger's seat.

"Yes." Fadi opened the door and climbed in. Jane got in also and buckled her seatbelt. She wondered where Fadi was driving her to. Truly that man was full of surprises.

Fadi stuck the key in the ignition and started the engine. Jane sat there silently for about ten seconds. "Where are we going?" she asked.

"To my office," he said.

So many questions swarmed Jane's mind. Why were they going to the office? Was he giving her more work? Why her when he had more experienced people?

"I can hear your mind," said Fadi as he stopped at a traffic light. He turned his head and looked at her.

"What do you mean?" Jane asked.

"You have questions to ask me."

Jane opened her mouth. Why was he getting so good at reading her? When she couldn't read him. Fadi held her gaze. She couldn't hold his gaze any longer. He made her nervous. His gaze reminded her of the kiss they had shared. Jane looked away.

"Why are we going to your office?" she asked. The traffic light turned green and Fadi drove off.

"I want to show you around."

That did not answer her question. Jane sighed and just sat back in her seat. Fadi was not the type of person who divulged information when asked. She just needed to be patient. He was going to tell her when they arrived.

Fortunately, they arrived at the office no more than ten minutes later. After they parked, Jane and Fadi got out of the car. They walked through the automatic glass doors and into the lobby of the office. They walked across the white floor and headed over to the elevators. The security guards greeted Fadi cheerfully.

"This place is even open during the weekend," Jane commented as they walked into the elevator. Fadi pressed the buttons.

"Of course. Why wouldn't it be?" Fadi replied.

"Because it's a weekend."

Fadi looked at her with a blank expression. Jane sighed and shook her head. Obviously, he did not understand that people should rest during the weekend since he did not rest during the weekend. He worked. A lot.

Fadi gave Jane a tour of the building. He showed her where the geology department was, oil and gas department, finance, human resources and he showed her the fancy technology used to build models for reservoirs. Jane was incredibly impressed. The offices were clean and expensive-looking. She could see why her classmates wanted to work there.

Lastly, they went to see Fadi's office. He opened the door and held the small of her back and ushered her in. Jane's eyes flew wide open. He touched her back so naturally as if it was something he did all the time. Jane was confused by him. She could not figure him out.

Jane quickened her step to escape his touch. She wasn't surprised that his office was clean and tidy and furnished with white furniture. That was the only predictable thing about him. She stood in front of Fadi's desk and looked outside the large windows.

"Your offices are impressive," said Jane as she slipped her hands into her pockets. Fadi stood between Jane and his desk. He leaned against it, not that there was much space. His long legs nearly touched hers. Fadi folded his arms over his chest.

"Do you have any skirts or dresses?" he asked.

"Huh?" Jane frowned.

"When you weren't in your uniform, I've seen you in clothes..." He scanned her from head to toe. "Like this," he finished.

"Clothes like what? It's getting cold out there. It is only natural to wear tracksuits." Jane crossed her eyebrows. "But why are we discussing my clothes?" she asked.

"From now on, I want you to work here or at my house, wherever I am. I will need you to attend meetings with me and so I need you to dress appropriately," he explained. Jane ran her hand through her hair. More questions flooded her mind.

"Work with you?" she asked.

"You are talented and I don't want your talents to be wasted on being my maid."

"So you want me to work here?!" she cried out in excitement. That she had not seen coming.

"I won't ask if you're excited," he said. A soft giggle bubbled from Jane's throat.

"Thank you." That was the best thing he had done for her. It was the first step she was taking towards her career.

"I want you to be working with me on my refinery," he said. Jane grinned. She was going to be working on a new refinery. Not working at one that was already up and running, but a brand-new one. It was not an opportunity that came often. She knew that she was going to have to work very hard and assure Fadi that he had made the right decision in recruiting her.

"Are you sure about this? You are aware that I have no formal experience?" she said.

"If your performance is not up to par, you will just have to go back to being my maid."

Jane's facial expression quickly turned serious. He could at least have said that they would take it slowly or he would give her all the help she needed. Just something to reassure her.

"I will still work my weekend hours?" She couldn't afford to work more shifts because of her classes at the university.

"Yes." Fadi unfolded his arms and touched her waist. "I just can't have you wearing things like this," he said.

He headed for the door. Jane curled her upper lip. She was sure that he was teasing her. He had touched her for like a second and then walked off. What was that about? Couldn't he touch her for longer?

Chapter 17

Jane

"What the hell?" Jane mumbled as she followed Fadi into an expensive boutique. The type of boutique that no one could just walk into. You had to ring the doorbell and be invited in. The type of boutique she would walk past because one blouse was enough to pay for a year of her rent.

"Good afternoon, sir." A woman neatly dressed in a suit greeted Fadi. "Ma'am," she said to Jane.

"Hello," Jane replied.

"How may I help you? Are you looking for anything specific?" she asked. Jane wondered too. She looked at Fadi for answers.

"Can you find me your finest formal dresses and skirts in her size?" Fadi asked her.

"What?" Jane spat out. They were there for her.

"Yes sir," the woman replied. She walked off and started roaming around in the boutique picking out clothes.

"I have formal clothes of my own," Jane said to Fadi. He looked at her with a blank expression. He did not believe her. "I do. Let's go." She turned on her heel but Fadi caught her arm and spun her around. Jane let out a small squeak.

"I want to buy clothes for you that will be fitting for the work environment and meetings with high-profile clients," he said to her.

"I have appropriate clothes," she spat out. Fadi said nothing. "Why are you doubting me? You don't know what is in my closet."

Fadi looked at her from head to toe. Jane sighed heavily with a frown. He was a stubborn man determined to get his way. The store assistant re-approached them with a few clothes.

"I have picked out a few items for you. Would you like to try them on?" she said.

"Yes," Fadi answered faster than Jane could refuse. On the rare occasions that she went shopping for herself, she did not try the clothes on in the store. Now she had to, in front of Fadi. She looked at him from the corner of her eyes and frowned a little.

"Please follow me," the store assistant said. Jane reluctantly followed.

The first thing Jane tried on was a grey pencil skirt and a white blouse. She also screamed when she saw the prices of the two items. Together they cost $3,000. Where they made of gold or something?

"Are you going to come out?" she heard Fadi's voice call out. Jane opened the door and jerked her head out. Fadi was sitting on the sofa a few feet away from the changing room.

"Do I have to show you?" she asked. He waved her over. He scanned her from head to toe and then nodded in approval.

"Go try another," he ordered her. Jane frowned as she returned to the changing room.

"What a fussy man," she mumbled to herself. Next she tried on a burgundy pencil dress. It clung to her curves or rather lack of curves. Jane pouted at her reflection in the mirror. A dress like that would suit Regina better.

Jane walked out of the changing room and went to show Fadi the dress. She couldn't believe that she was in such a situation. Her boss was buying her clothes and watching her try them on.

"Here," she said. She stood right in front of him with her hands dangling at her sides. Fadi looked at her and said nothing for a moment. His gaze slowly washed over her. Silence stretched between them. Jane was starting to feel awkward.

"I don't think this one would be appropriate for work," he said.

"Huh?" Jane turned to face the full-length mirror on the wall to her right. "There is nothing wrong with it," she said. It did not reveal much. Yes, it was a little tight but she did not have a lot of curves.

Fadi rose to his feet and stood behind Jane. She looked at him in the mirror. He was already looking at her. He reached out and lightly touched her waist. "Are you sure?" he asked her. He traced her hips with his hands.

"Yes." Her voice came out more high-pitched than she wanted. It was hard to maintain composure when he was touching her. He caressed her side so gently before he pulled her closer to him. He pressed his chest into her back. The last time her back was against his chest, he had kissed her. Finally! It was about to happen again. Jane rubbed her lips together, just to wet them a little. It had been hours since she had used lip balm. She couldn't have dry lips when Fadi kissed her.

"I brought a dress that you migh..." The store assistant stopped speaking halfway and gasped. "I am sorry to interrupt," she said. Fadi pulled away from Jane and looked at the woman. Jane narrowed her eyes. Nooo! She had interrupted a moment she had been waiting for.

"No worries," Fadi said to her and took the dress. He gave it to Jane. "Try this on," he said to her. Jane took it and returned to the changing room. She placed her hands where Fadi's hands had been. She giggled quietly. He had such strong warm hands.

After trying on the clothes, Jane and Fadi went to pay for the items at the cash register. Jane was shocked to see bagged shoes. Fadi already picked out shoes for her.

"That will be a total of $15,500," said the woman. Jane gasped so loudly, both Fadi and the store assistant looked at her.

"That is quite expensive," she said.

"Our clothes are made with real silk, real wool and many other fine fabrics. I can assure you that the price is worth it," the store assistant said to Jane. Fadi did not say anything. He just whipped his bank card out of his wallet and paid for everything so easily. To him, $15,500 must have been equal to pocket change but to Jane, that was a lot of money.

"I'll carry them," Jane said to Fadi when he picked up all the shopping bags.

"You have poor upper body strength. It's best I do it," he replied. Jane frowned at him as he headed for the door. She hissed before she followed him out. Fadi put the shopping bags in the trunk of the car. Jane waited in the passenger's seat.

When he was done, Fadi joined her in the car. "Where do you live?" he asked as he stuck the key in the ignition.

"You want to take me home?" she asked.

"Yes. I have to meet someone soon."

"Okay." Jane put her address in the navigator.

It was a quick and short ride home. When they arrived, Fadi got out of the car and took out the shopping bags. "I'll bring them up for you," he said.

"I can carry them," Jane replied.

"No you can't. Lead the way."

Jane frowned a little. She could have carried the bags. They headed to the elevator. Jane pressed the button for the fifth floor.

When they reached her door, Fadi put the shopping bags on the floor.

"Thank you, but you did not have to do all of this," said Jane.

"Tomorrow will be your last shift as my maid. Next Friday, just come to my house as per usual and await my instructions," he said.

"Okay," Jane replied. Fadi reached out and touched one wayward tendril that resisted and now was in Jane's face.

"And brush your hair," he said.

"I did," Jane spat out. "It was just windy when I left," she mumbled. Fadi grunted in response. He turned on his heel and walked off. Jane sighed as she watched him walk off. He sent her so many mixed signals. When he touched her waist, that was the perfect moment to kiss her but then he did not. Just what was going on in his head?

Jane unlocked the front door and took the shopping bags in. Regina was just walking out of the kitchen when she saw her.

"You went shopping?" Regina asked. "You hate shopping, and you were meant to be at work."

"Sheikh Asaad bought all this for me," said Jane as she kicked the front door shut with her heel.

"He what? Why? Jane, why?"

Jane started laughing at Regina's reaction. "That's not even the most shocking part of it all," she said.

"What happened? Tell me everything, from the beginning."

Jane knew that she had to come clean about the kiss. She couldn't hide the kiss from Regina and she wanted some advice. Regina understood men more than Jane.

"Help me take these to my room and I'll tell you," said Jane. Regina helped her carry the bags to her bedroom. Then they sat on Jane's bed as Jane told Regina everything. Regina gasped and hit Jane on the arm.

"He kissed you and you never said anything? For a week?" Regina cried out.

"I'm sorry but I just couldn't believe it. I don't know why he kissed me."

"Well, obviously because he is attracted to you."

"He sure has a funny way of showing it."

"He gave you a job at his oil company and bought you clothes. I'd say he is pretty clear about his feelings," said Regina.

"I don't know. I can't tell." Jane buried her head in her hands. Regina burst into laughter.

"When in doubt either confront him about it…"

"NO! Absolutely not!" Jane cut Regina off and flat-out refused. There was no way she was going to talk to Fadi about the kiss and practically tell him how she felt.

"Or just go with the flow, you coward," Regina finished. Yes, Jane was a coward. Not by choice but because of her lack of experience with men. It was best for her to just watch the situation play itself out.

Chapter 18

Fadi

Fadi was in his home office trying to go over a finance report for one of the reservoirs but he couldn't concentrate. His mind kept playing over the events of the previous day. He could still remember Jane in her burgundy dress. He wanted to hold her body tightly against his and kiss her. He chastised himself for feeling that way because he was betrothed to another.

He had never wanted to kiss Faiza but he had found himself wanting to kiss Jane a lot. When he returned from Al Hamri, he wanted to pick up where they had left off but he had stopped himself. It was best that they did not kiss again.

There was a knock on the door. "Come in," he called out. The door swung open and Jane walked in.

"Good afternoon," she said as she walked over to his desk and stood across from him. She never came to greet him whenever she came to work. She just arrived and started cooking and cleaning. She would only call him to eat.

"You are greeting me today." Fadi was amused.

"You are always working, and so I never wanted to disturb you."

It was a poor excuse. "I'm working now," he said. Jane narrowed her gaze.

"What would you like to eat for lunch?" she asked.

"You never asked me that either."

"Well, it is my last day."

"Your hair is back to being wavy," said Fadi. Jane touched her ponytail.

"Oh, you noticed," she said.

"Was your change in hairstyles meant for my attention?"

"No! Why would it be?" she spat out. Her response made him suspicious. He had asked her as a joke but she was overreacting. It was as if he was correct. "I am going to make you rice and lamb," she said. She turned so fast, her hip hit his desk and caused her to stumble back a little.

"Ow!" she cried out. Fadi shook his head as he rose to his feet. He walked around the table and stood in front of her.

"Jane, why are you so clumsy?" he asked.

"If I could answer that question, then I would have a solution to my clumsiness," she spat out. Fadi touched her hip where she had hurt herself and started rubbing. Jane flinched. She tried to take a step back but Fadi held her waist with his other hand.

"Stay still," he said as he kept on rubbing her hip.

"I could have rubbed it myself," she mumbled.

"Where were you trying to go so fast?" Fadi wanted to laugh. Jane flared her nostrils. She folded her arms over her chest and looked away. Fadi placed both hands on her waist and pulled her closer to him. He inhaled her subtle sweet scent. She did not wear too much perfume like Mariam did. He suspected that Jane's scent came from bath soaps.

"I think my hip is fine now," she said without looking at him. Fadi cupped her chin and turned her face to face him. She raised her eyebrows and searched his eyes. She dropped her arms to her sides. Fadi moved his face closer to hers and placed his lips over hers. Ah, the softness of her lips. How he had missed it. Fadi slowly kissed her. Jane just stood there with her arms at her sides and her eyes closed.

Fadi broke off the kiss and watched Jane slowly open her eyes. "I must be the first men you've ever kissed," he said. Jane crossed her eyebrows and pushed him away from her.

"No you're not!" she said. Fadi raised his eyebrows.

"Then why are you reacting like that?" She was so animated. Fadi found it so amusing.

"I kissed other men before you."

"Really?" He did not believe her. He could tell by the way she responded or rather didn't respond to his kisses. She did not know what to do with her hands or lips. Jane opened her mouth to say something but before the words came out, Fadi's office door swung open and in walked his little sister.

"Fadi!" she screeched. Fadi raised an eyebrow. What the hell was she doing there? She had a habit of surprising people.

"What are you doing here?" he asked her.

"Is that how you are going to greet me after all this time we've been separated?"

"Amina, it's only been one week."

Jane stood there awkwardly with red cheeks. Amina looked at her. "Hi?" she said.

"Hello," Jane replied.

"Who is she?" Amina asked Fadi.

"I work for the sheikh."

"This is Jane," said Fadi.

"Um, shall I make lunch for you as well?" Jane asked Amina.

"Yes. I will be staying over for a while," Amina replied.

"What?" Fadi spat out. Jane nodded and excused herself. "Why are you here?" Fadi asked his sister after Jane had left the room.

"Can't I come and spend some quality time with my brother?" she said. Fadi rolled his eyes.

"Aren't you meant to be in school?" he asked. She was only in her first year at the university.

"I'm on holiday," she grinned at him.

***

Jane

Jane was full of mixed emotions as she prepared lunch for Fadi and his female visitor. Jane wanted to know who the burgundy-haired girl was. She had burst into Fadi's office as if it were her own. Clearly she was someone important to Fadi because he did not seem angry about her barging in.

Jane was also confused by Fadi's actions once again. He teased her and kissed her and teased her again. She had waited for that second kiss for what had felt like a million years and that moment was quickly ruined when Fadi asked her if he was the first man to kiss her. She felt so embarrassed that he knew. She must have been a really bad kisser for him to be able to tell just like that. When he asked her, Jane just wanted the ground to open up and swallow her.

It was always awkward serving Fadi food but this time it was a hundred times worse. Jane had to serve him and the burgundy-haired girl who couldn't seem to stop looking at Jane.

She was sitting comfortably at the table looking at Jane with such curiosity. She was about three inches shorter than Jane. She had smooth olive skin. She was slim but she had curves. More than Jane. Everyone had more curves than Jane. She had big hazel eyes, a perfectly straight nose and medium-sized lips. Her face was perfectly contoured. Jane couldn't tell if it was makeup or natural.

"How old are you? You seem quite younger than all the other maids here," the girl finally asked her.

"Twenty-five," Jane replied as she poured out drinks for them.

"Oh, that is quite young."

"Amina, leave her alone," Fadi warned.

"Am I bothering you, Jane?" Amina asked her.

"No." Jane forced a smile. She was. Jane was bothered by her. She wanted to know just who she was and why she was so curious about Jane.

"You are dismissed. You may return to the kitchen," Fadi said to Jane. She raised her eyebrows. He never dismissed her when he ate. He always wanted her there, standing by the door. She did not like it but this time she wanted to stick around. Why was he getting rid of her?

"Is there anything I could get you before I leave?" Jane asked.

"No," Fadi replied. Jane nodded and left the room. She returned to the kitchen and started cleaning. She just wanted the day to fly by. She no longer wanted to be there with Fadi and his mystery woman. Amina. She was beautiful. She was quite the opposite of Jane.

"Jane!" she heard Amina call out. Her voice was quite high-pitched. Jane reluctantly headed to the dining room. The last thing she wanted was to get orders from Fadi's woman.

"Yes, miss," Jane said as she walked into the dining room.

"Oh please, call me Amina," she said with a smile.

"Okay, how can I assist you?" Jane replied.

"Your food tastes amazing."

"Thank you." Jane wondered if that was why she had called her.

"How long have you worked for Fadi?" she asked.

"Why do you want to know?" Fadi asked her.

"I am just asking her."

"I have worked here for about two months," Jane replied. Indeed, why did she want to know?

"It must be hard to work for my brother. He can be so fussy and uptight," said Amina.

"Brother?" Jane asked. She tried to mask her excitement but she suspected that she failed because Fadi raised his eyebrows and looked at her in amusement.

"Yes." Amina laughed. "Who did you think I was to him?"

"No one. I didn't give it a thought. It's none of my business," Jane lied. She felt so relieved and was suddenly feeling very friendly towards Amina. She did not mind answering all her questions.

"We will be going out for dinner tonight, so you don't have to cook," Fadi said to her. "You can leave early today."

"Thank you for letting me know," Jane replied. Fadi rose to his feet and walked out of the dining room. Amina rose to her feet also.

"I'll see you later, Jane." She smiled and walked out also. Jane smiled and sighed with relief. It was just his sister.

Chapter 19

Jane

It was already midday but Jane was still rolling around in bed. She had been studying into the night, and so she had slept very late. She heard the doorbell ringing. She ignored it at first, since she was not expecting anyone but then it rang again. She growled as she stumbled out of bed in nothing but an oversized T-shirt. She swung the door wide open.

"What the hell?" she said when she saw Fadi standing in front of her.

"My words exactly," he said as he looked at her from head to toe.

"What are you doing here?"

"I have a meeting at 2 and I thought you might want to come."

Jane narrowed her gaze at him. "That would be nice but couldn't you give me a call or something?" she asked. Fadi shrugged his shoulders unapologetically.

Jane sighed. "I will get ready," she said. Fadi decided to let himself into her apartment.

"Hurry up," he said. Jane opened her mouth and screamed silently. She was embarrassed to be seen in such a state. Her hair was messy and she was in nothing but a T-shirt.

"Okay." Jane dashed to the bathroom and had a quick shower. She went back to her bedroom and fished out one of the outfits he had bought for her. She wore a white pencil skirt and a silk camisole. She added a pair of black high heels with red soles. She brushed her hair and tied it up into a neat ponytail.

"I'm ready," she said as she entered the living room where Fadi was seated so comfortably as if he was in his own house.

"You couldn't even give me a tour of your place," he said to her. Jane burst into laughter.

"You came over unannounced."

Fadi rose to his feet. He was wearing a pair of navy-blue trousers, sky-blue shirt and a navy-blue suit jacket. His week-old beard was neatly shaped. He was such a good-looking man.

"You get your blue eyes from your mother?" said Fadi.

"Huh?" Jane was confused by the quick change of subject. "Oh, yes I do." She looked at the picture of her parents on the wall.

"Do you have any siblings?" he asked her.

"No, it's just me."

"Must be peaceful."

"Why?" she asked.

"My siblings are so annoying."

Jane smiled. "I thought Amina was sweet," she said.

"Before or after you found out that she was my sister?"

"Both, before and after."

Fadi raised his eyebrows and smiled a little. "You thought she was my woman," he said.

"I did not, and even if she was, it has nothing to do with me," said Jane.

"Yours actions speak louder. You were so relieved when you found out who she was."

"We need to leave if we are to make that meeting in time," said Jane as she headed for the door. Damn. Once again Fadi had seen right through her. There was no point in denying the truth or lying to him. He always caught her. He knew her thoughts a little too well. Jane heard Fadi laugh behind her as she walked off. She frowned and growled silently. It was so embarrassing.

Jane felt like someone very important as she walked into a large conference room with Fadi at her side. It was going to be her first ever professional meeting. She was excited. There were other men in the room already when they entered. She recognized the tall, handsome man dressed in a navy-blue suit. It was

Sofian. He recognized her also. He offered a warm smile when their eyes met. Jane returned his smile.

"This is Jane, my assistant," Fadi said to them. "She is a master's student at MIT."

"MIT, whoa. Beauty and brains," said one man with a smile. He was tall but not as tall as Fadi. His brown hair was cut short on the back and sides. He had piercing grey eyes. He extended his hand to Jane. "Roman Waters," he said.

"Waters, as in CEO of Dallas Oils?" she asked.

"Guilty." He shrugged his shoulders. Jane's face lit up.

"Wow, it's so good to meet you." She shook his hand.

"I take it you know of our work," he said with a smile.

"Of course I do. Your company produces the best drilling machinery," she said.

"Jane was the one who recommended your drills to us," Fadi said.

"Is that so?" Roman smiled. Jane smiled back.

Fadi's lawyers and Roman's lawyers negotiated the terms of their contract. Roman and Fadi were about to sign a contract together. Fadi wanted Roman's company to provide them with all the drilling equipment they needed. Fadi also wanted Dallas Oils to provide some equipment for the Asaad Refinery.

During the meeting, Jane caught Roman looking at her a few times. Jane just looked away. She did not know what else to think or do. He probably was just curious about her or something. She stole a glance at Fadi. He was sitting next to her. He looked so regal and professional. He made her heart flutter.

The meeting adjourned after the contracts were signed. Fadi left Jane's side and went to speak to Sofian. Roman approached Jane.

"So, what is your master's in?" he asked her.

"Petroleum refining systems," she replied. Roman nodded with approval.

"That is not an easy course."

"No it isn't, but it's interesting."

Roman and Jane talked more about her master's. He seemed quite interested and impressed by her educational background. He pulled out a business card from his pocket and handed it to Jane.

"You should give me a call sometime," he said to Jane. "You might be interested in coming to Dallas Oils just to look around or even to apply for a job after your graduation."

"Oh wow." Jane looked at the business card. "Thank you." She slipped it into her handbag. Fadi finished up with the lawyer and then went over to Jane. He bid his farewell to Roman, and then he left the conference room with Jane.

"Did you want me to attend the meeting because I first mentioned Dallas Oils to you?" Jane asked Fadi as they headed towards the elevator.

"Yes," he replied.

"Good afternoon, Sheikh Asaad," a woman said as she walked past with a big smile on her face. Fadi just nodded in response.

"Thank you for letting me attend," Jane said to him.

"Sure."

The elevator doors were closing as they arrived. One of the women inside put her hand between the doors to stop it from closing so that Jane and Fadi could catch the elevator.

"Thank you," Jane said to her, but she suspected that it wasn't for her. The woman was staring at Fadi with a smile on her face.

"Hello, Sheikh Asaad," she said. Fadi gave her a nod and slipped his hands in his pockets. Jane noticed that he never greeted people. She waited until they were out of the elevator and in his car before she asked him about it.

"Sir, whenever people greet you, why don't you reply?" Jane asked him. It was kind of rude.

147

"What are you talking about?" he asked her.

"You just nod, like this." Jane imitated him.

"Shall I embrace them then?" he asked. Jane laughed and shook her head.

"Just say hello. It doesn't hurt and it will not cost you anything."

"What were you and Roman talking about?" Fadi changed the subject.

"Huh?" Jane wondered why he was asking.

"The two of you seemed to be in a very interesting conversation." Fadi's tone suggested that he wasn't all that pleased but Jane could not tell if he was jealous because she worked for him or because he had feelings for her.

"I did not even know that you were paying attention," she said.

"I wasn't. I just noticed."

"He gave me his business card."

Fadi turned and looked at her. "Are you going to call him?" he asked.

"Do you mind?" She wanted him to say, *Yes I mind, you're mine and I don't want you anywhere near him*. She wanted him to just say something that made her know how he felt towards her.

"No. You can call him if you want," Fadi replied. Jane looked away. His answer disappointed her. There was silence in the car for the rest of the journey back to her apartment. Jane did not like being uncertain.

They reached Jane's apartment and parked outside. "I'll see you on Friday," he said to her. Jane turned and faced him.

"Why do you keep giving me mixed signals?" she asked him. She had kept the question in long enough.

"What?" he said so calmly.

"I lost my temper at the interview but you hired me anyway. You were always so cold to me but then you gave me development plans to work on. You kissed me and then acted as though nothing had happened." Jane sighed. She could feel herself getting angry. Fadi just stared at her. He looked amused. It was making her even more angry.

"Are you done?" he asked.

"This is not funny."

"I never said it was."

"You look incredibly amused right now," she spat out. "I am not even experienced enough to be working at your company. I heard that you usually hire people with ridiculously high grades and tons of experience. Why me?"

"You are smart," he said. Jane sighed. She was not getting anywhere with him. Clearly he was not telling her everything.

"Fadi," she said. He raised his dark eyebrows in shock when she said his name. She never called him by his first name but it just slipped out of her mouth. "Stop sending me mixed signals. Be clear with your intentions."

Fadi responded by moving closer to her and kissing her. It was a quick and passionate kiss. Jane froze in place. The pleasure made her forget just what she was saying before the kiss.

"Now that you have stopped yelling at me," he said. "You are different to every woman I have ever met. You aren't afraid to speak your mind. I need honest people I can trust around me, and I think you are quite smart and have the potential to be one of the best engineers."

"Um, okay," Jane said quietly. He definitely knew how to shut her up. He had kissed her and then complimented her. He never complimented her. She had to look outside to check if the sky was falling.

Fadi cupped her chin and stroked her jawline with his thumb. He leaned forward and pressed a kiss against her lips. "I have other matters to attend to. Can I go, that is if you're finished scolding me?" he said.

Jane slowly nodded. She was still reeling from the pleasure of his kiss. She opened the door and climbed out of the car. She stumbled a little as she got out.

"Be careful," Fadi said to her. She could sense the smile in his words. Why did she always have to trip in front of him? She needed to learn how to walk properly.

"Bye," she said and quickly headed into the building.

Chapter 20

Jane

Regina and Jane headed to Starbucks for some coffee before they both went to work. It was getting really cold, and so it was the perfect time for a hot mocha. Jane loved mocha. That combination of chocolate and coffee was heavenly.

"Can we get a large mocha and a large latte please?" Jane said to the barista who looked about 20 years old.

"Would you like anything else?" he asked. Jane scanned the sweet treats through the thick glass.

"That slice of red velvet looks good," she said. "Do you want one?" she asked Regina.

"No," she replied.

"Charge it on this card," Jane heard a voice sound from behind her. She and Regina both turned. Jane saw Roman standing behind her. He smiled and stood next to her.

"Can you add a medium latte to that?" he said to the barista as he passed him his bank card.

"Thank you, Mister…?" said Regina.

"Mr. Waters," said Jane with a smile. "Thank you, sir."

"Please call me Roman." He winked. Regina and Jane both smiled at him. The barista handed Roman his bank card before he disappeared to prepare their orders.

"Fancy meeting you here," Jane said to him. Roman smiled.

"I am on my way to a meeting but decided to stop by for some coffee. What are you ladies up to?"

"Coffee before work."

"I am leaving for Dallas tomorrow evening. Let's grab some lunch tomorrow."

"I will be working," Jane replied.

"No worries, we can grab breakfast instead," he said. "We can talk more business."

"Sure. I guess we can just meet here."

"Does 10 o'clock work for you?"

The barista returned with their order.

"Ten is fine," Jane said as she reached out for her mocha.

"See you tomorrow." Roman touched Jane's arm lightly. He smiled and nodded at Regina before he left. Regina grabbed her latte.

"He's handsome. Who is he?" she said.

"Roman Waters. I met him on Wednesday at the meeting Fadi took me to," she said. She took a sip of her mocha.

"I hope you realize that he wanted to take you on a date." Regina wiggled her eyebrows as they both walked off from the cashier.

"What? Where did you get that from?"

"He asked to have lunch with you." Regina pushed the glass doors open and walked out of the café.

"To talk business," Jane explained.

"Oh please. That was an excuse."

"I doubt it." She really did. That was her they were talking about. She wasn't so lucky with men.

"Trust me on this one. Roman is taken by you. Did you not see how he touched your arm before he left?"

"I am sure he was being friendly."

Regina burst into laughter. "Fadi would not think so," she said. Jane sighed.

"Fadi is a piece of work," she replied.

"Or maybe it's you that is a piece of work."

"Why me?"

"You miss the signs and then you blame him for giving you mixed signals."

"What?" Jane whipped her head in Regina's direction. "I assure you that I am not the problem."

Regina smiled. "I am just teasing you, sort of," she said. "He does give you mixed signals but I do think that he likes you but you are missing his signs. Maybe he is just not the type of man to stand with a flashing sign saying how much he likes you."

"I wish he would because otherwise I would not know how he feels about me," Jane replied right before she took a huge bite out of her red velvet cake. Regina handed her a tissue to wipe the cream from her face.

"I have to go. Have fun at work." Regina wiggled her eyebrows mischievously before she walked off. Jane walked off in the opposite direction and went to catch her bus to Fadi's house.

She arrived at work right on time as usual. She stood outside the front door for a moment, wondering what the day had in store for her. She wondered what work Fadi was going to give her.

"Hi Jane," she heard a voice sound from behind her. It was so high-pitched she knew who it was. Amina.

Jane turned around. "Hi Amina," she said to her.

"How are you?"

"I'm fine. How are you?" She was different to her brother. Fadi never asked Jane how she was.

"I'm okay. Aren't you going in?" Amina pushed the front door open and walked into the house.

"I was about to," Jane said as she followed Amina in. Jane was itching to ask Amina about Fadi but she did not know how to do it without being so obvious. "You and the sheikh seem close," she said.

"We are." Amina smiled at Jane. The two of them headed towards Fadi's office. "But we are quite different. He works too much and I party too much."

"I agree; he works too much." Jane took her jacket off and hung it on her arm.

"You're dressed quite formally," Amina pointed out. "You look nice."

"Thank you." Jane straightened her green silk camisole.

When they reached Fadi's office, Amina opened the door as casually as if she was walking into her own bedroom. Fadi looked up from his desk and watched Amina walking in. Jane followed behind her.

"Why are the two of you coming in together?" he asked.

"We ran into each other at the front door." Amina plonked herself on Fadi's desk. He shook his head.

"Good evening sir," Jane greeted Fadi. The first two buttons on his shirt were unbuttoned, revealing some of that almond-colored toned chest.

"Hello Jane," he replied. Wow, her words had not fallen on deaf ears. She had talked to him about ignoring people when they greeted him. Apparently, he had listened to her because he greeted her.

"She looks so smart, doesn't she?" Amina said to Fadi about Jane.

"She does," Fadi agreed. Jane clutched her bag. She felt awkward. She was used to coming into work and cooking but now she had to wait for instructions.

"There is a weird vibe between the two of you."

"What do you mean?" Jane asked.

"I don't know. It's as if you were a couple in your past life or something."

What! Jane raised her eyebrows. That was rather random but it had some truth in it. Maybe not a couple in their past life but there was some attraction between herself and Fadi. Could Amina sense it?

"Why are you here?" Fadi asked his sister. She smiled and jumped off his desk.

"I am leaving, don't worry." Amina slammed the door on her way out. Jane cleared her throat.

"What would you like to do with me today?" she asked Fadi.

"A lot of things." He had a mischievous look on his face.

"Excuse me?"

Fadi rose to his feet and picked up some paperwork. He walked over to the white sofas in his office. "Come sit here," he said to Jane. He sat down and put the paperwork on the glass table. Jane hesitated for a moment. Then she went to join him at the sofas. She sat on the sofa opposite him.

"Here." He touched the seat next to him. Jane swallowed hard before she went to sit next to him. Fadi watched her walk over and sit down.

"What's that?" She pointed at the paperwork. Jane needed to say something. She had to say anything to stop him from looking at her like that. His dark gaze made her knees weak.

"Have a read." He passed her a sheet of paper. Jane looked at it. It was about his refinery. Fadi explained to her that it was going to start running within one week. He wanted to import oil from Asaad Oil and refine it at his new refinery. He wanted to use his family oil to test out the refinery before accepting business from other companies.

"How many investors do you have for this refinery?" Jane asked Fadi.

"One," he replied.

"Just one?"

"Yes, me."

Jane gasped. "You paid for the entire thing with your money?" she asked.

"Yes." He shrugged his shoulders.

"Oh wow." That definitely cost him a fortune. Jane was shocked that he had enough money to build a refinery using his own money. "You are going to need to make that money back. That refinery needs to bring you high profits," she said.

"It will," he said.

"You sound very confident."

"I am."

"Once you refine oil into gasoline, diesel and other products, then what? Do you have buyers?" she asked.

"Yes. They will be sold to other companies," he replied. His gaze washed over her slowly. They were talking about something serious and here he was looking at her like that. It was alluring and distracting.

"How many lovers have you had in the past?" he asked.

"What does that have to do with anything?" Jane's eyes flew wide open.

"Zero?" he asked.

"That is none of your business," she replied.

"So it is zero then."

"That isn't what I said."

"You did not deny it."

"I have had a boyfriend before." Not this again. Why was he asking her?

"A boyfriend?" he asked.

"Boyfriends," she lied.

"Look at me," he demanded. Jane looked at him with her eyebrow raised. "I don't believe you," he said. Damn. Again he caught her in a lie.

"That is up to you. I don't really care."

"Kiss me."

"Why?" Jane frowned. As if she did not want to.

"Prove to me that I am not the only man you've ever kissed." He stared at her with such an intense gaze. Jane pecked him on the lips and quickly moved away.

"There," she said. Fadi snaked his arm around her waist and pulled her closer to him. She went flying to his chest. Jane pressed her palms against his chest. It felt so hard and warm.

Fadi held the back of her neck and pulled her head closer to him until their faces were touching. He parted her lips with his and kissed her slowly. Eek! Jane felt like she could fly. His kiss made her knees weak and her toes curl. He caressed her jawline with his thumb as he kissed her.

He pulled away and looked her right in the eye. "That's how you kiss," he said to her. Jane cleared her throat and distanced herself from him.

"Fine. You are the first man I've really kissed. So what?" she said. Pretending that she had kissed others was pointless because Fadi could tell that she hadn't. He surprised her by smiling about it.

"Good," he said.

"Why good?" Jane was confused.

"I can't imagine another man kissing you." He stroked her bottom lip with his thumb. Jane smiled and looked down. Suddenly there was a knock on the door. Jane jerked her head up and moved away from Fadi. She looked at the door. She wondered who that person was with bad timing.

"Who is it?" Fadi sounded annoyed. The door swung open and Amina poked her head through. "Since when did you start knocking?" he asked her.

"There is someone here to see you," she said with a smile. Fadi sighed.

"Who?" he asked. Amina opened the door wider, revealing a tall, slim but curvy woman with long, black silky hair and honey-colored skin. She had beautifully threaded eyebrows, long eyelashes, a straight nose, high cheekbones and perfectly sized lips. She wore a white bodycon dress and a pair of red high heels. She looked absolutely gorgeous and elegant.

"Your fiancée," Amina said.

Chapter 21

Jane

Jane walked through her front door and kicked it shut with her foot. She headed to the kitchen to make herself noodles. What else could she do? She had just found out that Fadi was engaged to another. She wanted an explanation from him and she also wanted to slap him for leading her on. However, when she saw Faiza, like a coward she had walked out of there without saying anything. She suspected that Amina knew that something was up because Amina had been looking at Jane suspiciously.

"You're home early," Jason said as he walked into the kitchen. Jane whipped her head in his direction and narrowed her gaze at him. He raised his eyebrows and stopped walking. "Jane?"

"Jason," she replied. He had done nothing wrong to her but she was not keen on talking to him. "Where is your girlfriend?"

"Um, she's in the bathroom. Are you okay?"

"You love her, don't you?"

"I do." Jason looked confused.

"You wouldn't lead her on or lie to her, would you?"

"Of course not, I would never do anything like that to her. Jane, what is going on? What's wrong?" Jason asked.

"Men," she spat out. She was obviously still angry over the incident with Fadi. She was angry and humiliated. She had been starting to believe that he liked her, at least a little bit. She definitely liked him, and was possibly falling for him. She felt like a darned fool.

"Regina, something is wrong. I don't know what to do," Jason said to Regina as she walked into the kitchen. The poor blameless man looked so confused after Jane had practically snapped at him.

"Something is wrong where?" Regina asked.

"With Jane."

Jane ran her hand through her hair. She could feel her eyes stinging

She was not going to cry. She refused to cry over him. "Fadi is engaged," Jane blurted out. Regina whipped her head in Jane's direction with her eyes widened.

"What?" she spat out.

"Who is Fadi?" Jason asked.

"I don't believe that. How did you find out?" Regina asked.

"She came over to the house. Faiza." Jane crossed her arms over her chest. "That's her name."

"And he told you that she was his fiancée?"

"Amina said she was his fiancée."

"Who is Amina?" Jason asked. He was really confused.

"My boss's sister," Jane replied.

"This Faiza, how old does she look?" Regina asked.

"She is about twenty-six or twenty-seven years old."

"She's Arabic too?"

"Yes. And she's beautiful. I can see why he would want to marry her."

"Stop it. I bet you are better than her."

"Except I'm not." She really wasn't. She paled in comparison. Faiza was beautiful.

"What did Fadi say to you?" Regina asked.

"Nothing. I didn't wait around to talk to him. I just left and now work will be awkward tomorrow," Jane replied.

"You're still going to work for him?"

"Of course I am. It's a good opportunity for me. I can't let it go to waste. I just have to put my big-girl panties on and get on with my job," she replied. It was easier said than done. She knew that it was going to be hard working with Fadi and pretending that nothing happened.

"Is Fadi the man you work for? And Faiza is his fiancée?" Jason asked.

"Yes," Jane and Regina said in unison. Jason raised his eyebrows.

"Okay, so why is it bad that he is engaged?" he asked. Regina and Jane looked at him as though he had lost his mind.

"Stop asking so many questions," Regina said to him.

"Ten seconds before Faiza walked in, Fadi had been kissing and flirting with me," said Jane. Jason's jaw hung open for a few seconds before he spoke.

"Something had been going on between Fadi and yourself," he stated the obvious. Well, not so obvious for him because he didn't know anything about Jane and Fadi kissing and flirting.

"Jason! You're so tactless. You'll make Jane feel bad," said Regina.

"We kissed a few times before," Jane said to Jason.

"And all this time he was engaged? Whoa. That's not good," he said.

"You think?" Regina said sarcastically.

"I'm sorry, Jane."

"I'm the fool here. I should have followed my gut. I knew that he was way out of my league," she said. It was too good to be true. There was no way a man like Fadi wanted a woman like Jane.

"He's not out of your league," said Jason.

"You can't say that. You don't know what he looks like or his background."

"Well, I know and I can say that he isn't out of your league because it's true," Regina spat out. She was only being a friend. However, that was true. Fadi was way out of Jane's league. He was handsome, tall and rich. He would obviously want to be with someone in the same social class.

"We should pay him a visit," said Regina. Jane knew that Regina meant to visit Fadi and give him a piece of her mind.

"No, there's no point," said Jane. Regina and Jason stared at her in shock.

"This is not the Jane I know," said Jason.

"I agree," said Regina. "When have you ever let things go?"

Good question. When had she ever let things go easily? Fadi was not going to get out of that situation unscathed. He had to explain why he wasn't more honest with her.

"I will give him a piece of my mind tomorrow," said Jane. She knew it possibly meant risking her job but it had to be done. She hoped that Faiza was nowhere in sight when she confronted Fadi. She'd lose her nerve if she had an audience. Jane put her noodles in the pot and switched the stove on.

"You're going to eat?" Jason asked.

"I'm not going to starve myself for anyone," she replied. Jason smiled.

"You're one of a kind."

Jane had to eat or do something to keep herself busy because if not, she was going to burst into tears. She really did not want to cry over Fadi. She was not going allow herself to.

The next morning, Jane wore the purple body-hugging dress that Fadi had bought for her. She let her long hair sit on her back. She didn't tie her hair up as she normally did. She put on a pair of black high heels that her mother bought for her but she never wore. She packed up all the clothes and shoes that Fadi bought for her. She was going to give them back to him and keep the purple one. The one he didn't want her to wear for anyone else.

"Wow, you look nice," Regina said to her as she walked out of her bedroom in pajamas.

"Thanks," Jane replied. She shut her bedroom door. "I'm going to have coffee with Roman before I go to Fadi's house."

Regina raised her eyebrows. "That Roman might have a crush on you, and if you turn up looking like that, he will definitely ask you out," she said.

"I don't think he's romantically interested in me."

"I think he is and you'll see. What's in those bags?"

"I'm taking these clothes back to Fadi." Jane headed for the front door.

She arrived at the Starbucks a few minutes later than the time she had agreed to meet with Roman. She wondered if he was a stickler for time like Fadi. Jane walked into the cafe and scanned the room. Roman was already seated at a table. He waved her over and rose to his feet as she approached.

"Wow," he said. He eyeballed Jane from head to toe. "You look amazing."

"Thank you," Jane replied.

Roman pulled out her chair. Jane awkwardly sat down. She wasn't used to people pulling out her chair for her. In fact, it had never happened before.

"What would you like to have?" Roman asked her.

"Just a mocha please." Jane smiled. Roman nodded and headed for the counter. Jane waited for his return. She wondered what he wanted to talk about with her. He returned shortly with their drinks.

"Thank you," Jane said as she reached out for her cup. She took a sip of the delicious hot liquid. The taste made her smile. "So what did you want to talk to me about?" She went straight to the point.

Roman smiled at her. He smiled so easily, unlike Fadi. Jane could probably count the amount of times she had seen him smile. "Straight to the point, huh. Okay, I'll do the same. I want you to work for me," he said. Jane almost choked on her mocha and coughed a little. Roman looked at her with concern.

"You want me to work for you?" she asked.

"Yes."

"Why? I have no experience. Why would you just want to hire me without knowing what I am capable of?"

"I looked you up. You graduated at the top of your class in your undergraduate degree. You are a very intelligent woman," he replied. Jane's eyebrows shot up.

"You looked me up?" That wasn't creepy at all.

"We had an interesting conversation when we first met, I wanted to know more about you."

"I may have graduated impressively but I still have no experience," she said.

"I have been in the oil and gas industry since I was twelve. I accompanied my father to meetings, oil rigs and I spent my weekends and holidays learning about my family's company. I know talent when I see it," he said.

"You think that I am talented?"

"Of course, I can see that you have the potential to become one of the best engineers. I'm sure even Sheikh Asaad thinks so."

"Sheikh Asaad? Why?"

"He hired you. He has a reputation for hiring the best of the best. He's very particular about who he hires."

Jane shrugged her shoulders. She knew that she was intelligent but it was all too good to be true. Both Fadi and Roman owned reputable companies. How could they both want to hire her without giving her an interview? At least Fadi had given her work before hiring her, so he had an idea of her capability.

"I will think about it," said Jane.

"Good. We can talk about it over dinner when I'm back in town." Roman winked at her. Jane widened her eyes.

"Dinner?" she asked. Roman smiled.

"I would like to take you out for dinner."

"For business?" It was important to clarify. She could remember Regina saying that Roman would ask her out.

"No. I think you're a beautiful woman and I would like to spend some time with you and get to know you."

Jane opened her mouth and then closed it. She didn't expect him to say that. He completely took her by surprise. She didn't know what to say.

"You have me at a loss for words." Jane took a few sips of her drink. Roman laughed a little.

"Think about both my offers. I'll be back in town next weekend. Give me a call and we can meet."

Chapter 22

Fadi

Breakfast was a quiet affair. Fadi sat there with Amina and Faiza. He wondered if Jane was going to show up for work. She had been predictable a lot of the time but this time he had no clue of what to expect. He hoped that she would come to work so that he could talk to her and explain. He didn't even know exactly what he would say to her. That he was engaged but didn't want to be? That he didn't love Faiza? The worst thing was that Faiza had decided to call him "my love" for the first time, right in front of Jane. Perfect.

"You're awfully quiet today," Faiza said to Fadi.

"He doesn't talk much usually," said Amina.

"Do your parents know that you are here?" Fadi asked Faiza. He suspected that they didn't know. Faiza was a princess and a single woman. Her parents wouldn't want her spending the night at a man's house, even if the man was her betrothed.

"They don't know," Faiza admitted shyly.

"Where do they think you are?" He asked.

"They are out of town for some more royal business. I have no interest in my father's affairs."

"You should return before they find out."

Faiza raised her eyebrows. "I wanted to see you," she said. "I still do. We have barely spent any time together."

"I understand but this isn't the proper time," Fadi said gently. Amina shot him a questioning glare. "I will be coming to Al Hamri soon. We can see each other then." He just wanted her to go back to her home.

"I was probably too impulsive," said Faiza.

"You just wanted to see your fiancé. It's natural," said Amina. She looked at Fadi and frowned at him a little.

"I will have my driver take you to the airport this afternoon." Fadi ignored his sister's glare. He rose to his feet. "If you could excuse me, I have matters to attend to," Fadi said before he walked out of the room. He headed to his office. He could not sit with Faiza and force a conversation. He wondered what it was going to be like when they got married. It was already so hard to hold a simple conversation with her.

Fadi shut his office door and sat down in his chair. He ran his hand through his short curly hair. His life was starting to get complicated. He had gotten himself into a complex situation. He was thinking about Jane more than he normally thought about any woman.

Suddenly his office door flew open and Amina walked in. She shut the door behind her and stood in front of Fadi's desk.

"Why are you so cold towards Faiza?" Amina asked him. Fadi frowned.

"I am just being myself," he replied. It was true. He was just being himself but he had often been told that he was cold. Jane had also told him that he was cold. Amina narrowed her gaze at him.

"It doesn't hurt to be nicer to her. She is going to be your wife," Amina spat out. Fadi said nothing. He just shrugged his shoulders. "She is going to be your wife, right?"

"I will try to be more considerate towards her," he said.

"What is happening between you and Jane?"

"What?" The question caught him off-guard.

"Yesterday when Faiza walked in, there was some kind of awkwardness. Both you and her got so weird." Amina squinted. She did that when she was trying to figure something out. "I can't put my finger on it but there is something between you and Jane," she finally said.

"I have no idea what you are talking about," he replied.

Amina sighed with frustration. "Fadi, you never want to talk to anyone about your thoughts. You need to stop blocking everyone out. I am your sister. You should talk to me," she said.

"I will come find you if I need to get something off my chest," he replied. He had to say that for her to calm down and leave him alone. He was also having a hard time explaining what he was feeling for Jane.

"Fine," she replied. There was a knock on the door. Fadi looked at the door with his gaze narrowed. It was probably Faiza coming to speak to him. Amina went to open the door. To him surprise, it was Jane. She stood at the door dressed in a gorgeous tight-fitting purple dress.

"Hi Jane," Amina greeted her cheerfully.

"Hi, how are you?" Jane replied.

"I'm fine." Amina opened the door wider for Jane to come in. Fadi watched her walking into his office. She looked absolutely gorgeous. She was holding a bunch of shopping bags. She placed them on the floor and just stood by his desk. Fadi stared at her. He was not sure what was going on.

He thought she was upset with him because of how she had left the night before. Part of him had assumed that she was not going to come to work.

However, she showed up on time and dressed so seductively. Jane had never worn a dress around him. She stood in front of his desk looking at him. Her big blue eyes looked different. Normally they were soft and innocent. This time, she had a fierce gaze. He couldn't tell if she was trying to seduce him or if she was angry at him.

"Um, I will leave the two of you to talk in private," Amina said awkwardly before walking out.

"I guess we do need to talk," Jane said to Fadi.

"Would you like to have a seat?" He gestured towards the tufted chair at his desk. Jane nodded and took a seat. "What are the bags for?" Fadi glared at the familiar shopping bags.

"I am returning the clothes you bought for me," she said. Fadi raised his eyebrows.

"Why?"

"I am sure that your fiancée would not appreciate you buying things for me," she replied as she leaned back in her chair.

"Are you upset about Faiza?"

"Of course I am!" she spat out. "Why did you not tell me?"

"I should have."

"Then why didn't you?"

"At first, you were just my employee and there was no reason to tell you about my personal life," he said. Jane frowned slightly. That was probably not what she wanted to hear but he wanted to be honest with her. "However, things got personal between us. It was not easy telling you," he added.

"I never thought that you would be such a dishonest man in a relationship."

Fadi was not surprised that Jane was confronting him. She was never one to hold her tongue. That was one of the things he liked about her. She was outspoken and honest.

"I am not a cheater," he said.

"Then what do you call kissing me behind your fiancée's back? It isn't fair to do that to the woman you love."

"Who said I love her?"

Jane rolled her eyes at him. "If you do not love her then why are you marrying her?" she asked.

"We were betrothed at a young age," he said. Jane opened her mouth and then closed it. She bit her lip.

"Betrothed, that is such an old word," she said. "So it is an arranged marriage?"

"Yes."

She shook her head. It was clear that she was in shock and was trying to digest the information he had given her. "Well, you are still engaged to her and kissing me was wrong," she said. She ran her hand through her hair.

"I can't change it." Fadi shrugged his shoulders.

"Change what, the engagement or kissing me?"

"Kissing you."

Jane raised an eyebrow. "This talk is not going anywhere." She sighed with frustration. "Am I some kind of toy to you?" she asked.

"No," he replied plainly. He had thought that if he explained the situation to her, she would be okay and just get over it. However, that wasn't the case. It was as if everything he said upset her further. Fadi was good at a lot of things but catering to people's emotions was not one of them.

Chapter 23

Jane

Jane was pissed. She had gone to speak with Fadi to get an explanation and somewhat clear the air but it wasn't going so well. It made her feel a little better knowing that his marriage to Faiza had been arranged. It meant that he had not fallen in love with her and then proposed to her. However, he was still going to get married to Faiza.

"Whatever. I am here to work. Let's just keep things professional," she said to him. She had asked him if he thought of her as some kind of toy and his answer was just no. He did not even bother to elaborate and say some words to make her feel better.

"You are still going to work for me?" he asked her in surprise.

"Yes. I am not going to throw away a good opportunity just because you decided to play with my feelings," she said. Fadi opened his mouth and stared at her in shock. "Although, Roman offered me a job," she added.

"Who is Roman?" Fadi asked with an eyebrow raised.

"Roman Waters."

"From Dallas Oils?"

"Yes."

Fadi frowned. "And what did you say?" His tone had changed.

"I said that I would think about it," Jane replied. Fadi rubbed his chin.

"When did he offer you the job?" His voice had gone deeper.

"I met up with him this morning."

"You went to see him in that dress?" he spat out. Jane's eyebrows shot up. She had never heard Fadi raise his voice. She suddenly remembered him saying that he did not want her to wear that dress for anyone other than himself. Was he jealous? No way.

"Yes," she replied. She wanted to test the waters and see if he really was jealous. "He also asked me out for dinner."

"What the hell?" Fadi sprung to his feet and started pacing. Jane stared at him in amusement. She wondered what was going through his mind.

"I told him that I would think about it."

He stopped walking and whipped his head in her direction. "What is there to think about?" he asked her.

"Well, I am a single woman. I can think about it if I wish to. I can even say yes."

"You will do no such thing."

Oh my! He was actually jealous. It was a side of him that she had not seen. He barely reacted to anything. This was the first time Jane saw him get angry and raise his voice. It was attractive. She wanted to dive into his arms and kiss him but then he was engaged to another.

"Excuse me, Sheikh Asaad." Jane rose to her feet. "You will not tell me what to do," she said. Fadi frowned again and walked over to her. He stood only inches away from her.

"You work for me. You will not take a job with him." His voice growled in his throat. He looked at her with such a dangerous expression. Jane felt shy and awkward but she was determined to stand her ground. She was not going to back down.

"I will decide what I wish to do with my future," she replied.

"You will not take him as your lover."

"Just because you said so?"

"Yes, because I said so."

"You are engaged or betrothed, whichever. You have no right to tell me what to do with my love life," she said. Fadi held her chin and pressed his lips to hers.

He kissed her so passionately and fiercely. It was so different to how he normally kissed her. There was something more fierce and possessive about this kiss.

It took Jane everything she had not to melt into his touch. She pushed him away from her and slapped his cheek with her right hand. Fadi touched his cheek and stared at her in shock.

"Do not play with my feelings like that," she said. She picked up her handbag and headed for the door. "Just e-mail me what you wish me to do and I'll work from home this weekend," she said. She opened the front door and walked out. She had thought that she could still work. Apparently not. She was so hurt and angry. Fadi hadn't even apologized. Instead he was all possessive over her. What a confused man!

Just before Jane walked out the front door, she saw Faiza coming down the stairs. She was wearing a long royal-blue dress. She looked beautiful.

"I met you yesterday," she said as she approached Jane. Jane stood by the front door and watched Faiza walk towards her.

"Yes. How are you?" Jane replied.

"I'm fine. What are you doing here?" She scanned Jane from head to toe.

"I work for the sheikh."

"During the weekend?"

"Yes. I work weekends only," Jane replied.

"Dressed like that?" she asked. Granted, Jane's dress was tight but it was knee-length and it did not reveal any cleavage.

"I am just on my way out. Is there something you wish to say to me?" Jane could sense the hostility in Faiza's questions.

"I just hope that you know your place."

Jane crossed her eyebrows. "My place?" she asked.

"I am the fiancée and you are the employee. Let us be clear about that," she warned.

Jane wanted to grab Faiza by the hair and throw her against the wall. However, that wasn't her style. Well, she did not know what her style was. She had never been in such a situation before. She did not know the appropriate way to act.

"You are a beautiful woman and you are already engaged to the sheikh. You should not be made to feel insecure by an ordinary skinny girl like myself," said Jane. If only Faiza knew that Fadi had just kissed her and practically claimed her as his no longer than two minutes ago.

"I do not like how you speak to me. Maybe you do not know this, but I am the only princess of Al Hamri. I would revise my speech if I were you," she said. Jane was shocked to learn that Faiza was a princess but she maintained a blank facial expression.

"As a princess, you should feel more secure and be nice to the peasants." Jane bowed her head, and then turned on her heel. She opened the front door and walked out of the house. She heard Faiza gasping but she did not bother to turn and look at her.

***

Jane marched to Regina's room when she arrived back at their apartment. She had so much to tell her best friend. She swung her bedroom door open.

"You would not believe what just happened to me today," Jane said as she walked into Regina's bedroom. Regina gasped as she sprang to her feet.

"You need to knock!" she said to her.

"You are dressed," she said to her. "Hi Jason," she greeted Regina's boyfriend. He was sitting on Regina's bed. He was wearing his boxer shorts and a T-shirt.

"Hey Jane," he replied. Regina tied her tight curls into a ponytail. She placed her hand on her hips.

"Why are you busting into my room like you do not have any manners?" Regina asked her.

"I went to have coffee with Roman," she said.

"Who is Roman?" Jason asked. Regina and Jane both turned to face him. "Jane just walked in on me in my boxer shorts and interrupted our kissing session. You might as well clue me into the conversation."

"Stay out of women's business," said Regina.

"His family owns Dallas Oils. It's a very successful company," Jane explained to Jason.

"Okay, and you went to have coffee with him?" Jason asked.

"He offered me a job."

"He did?" Regina's eyes flew wide open.

"That's good," said Jason.

"And then he asked me out for dinner," said Jane.

"I told you!" Regina cried out. Jane took her high heels off. Her feet were already hurting. She was not used to wearing high heels.

"Jane, you are a popular lady this month. Two job offers and two men are in love with you," said Jason.

"No one is in love with me," said Jane.

"This is why men should not be involved in girl talk," Regina said to her boyfriend as she shook her head.

"What did I do?" he asked.

"You say the wrong thing at the wrong time."

"I'm sorry, I was just being honest." Jason shrugged his shoulders.

Jane smiled. Jason and Regina were so adorable together. She hoped that she would have a relationship like that one day. It certainly did not seem like it was going to happen any time soon.

"Don't be sorry, Jason. I really do need a male opinion about this messy situation I have gotten myself into," said Jane. "Anyway, I went over to Fadi's house with the hopes of actually getting some work done."

Regina raised an eyebrow. "Like that was going to happen," she said.

"I just wanted to give him the stuff he bought for me, give him a piece of my mind and actually work."

"Then what happened?" Jason asked.

"I gave him the stuff back. I tried to give him a piece of my mind but he wasn't even apologetic, that bastard," said Jane. "He told me that he didn't love Faiza."

"Like that is believable." Regina rolled her eyes.

"Apparently, it is an arranged marriage."

"Oh wow." Regina's eyes flew wide open. "Well, it is common in his culture," she added.

"That still doesn't make the situation any better. Regina, he got so angry when I told him about Roman."

"Of course he did. Why wouldn't he?" said Jason.

"Well, he does a good job of convincing me that he does not care about me." Jane threw herself in the club chair in the corner of Regina's bedroom. "He demanded that I not work with Roman or go on a date with him," she said.

"Demanded?" Regina rolled her neck with so much attitude.

"He really does like you. He just doesn't know how to express his feelings," said Jason.

"I don't understand him," said Jane.

"Neither do I," said Regina.

"Shall we order some pizza?"

"You are thinking of food right now?"

"I am always thinking about food." Jane grinned. "Oh, and Faiza. I met her on my way out," she added. She explained to Jason and Regina what had happened with Faiza. Regina was obviously in disbelief.

"She is a princess? Well, that makes everything that much more complicated for you, Jane," said Jason as he rose to his feet. He rubbed Jane's head. "The least I could do for you is order the pizza." He offered a sympathetic smile.

"Thank you." She smiled.

"But, why don't you give Roman a chance?"

Regina and Jane both frowned at Jason.

"What?" Jason asked.

"The problem is that Jane wants Fadi. It's not that she just wants a man in general. So she can't just move on to the next available man," said Regina. She was very accurate.

"Okay, I will just go and order that pizza," he said helplessly.

Regina was quite right. Jane wanted Fadi and only him.

Chapter 24

Fadi

Fadi was sitting at the dining table when Sofian walked in. He looked at the silver Rolex sitting on his wrist. "You have never been good at being on time," Fadi said to him. Sofian shrugged his shoulders and smiled guiltily. He pulled out a leather chair and joined Fadi at the dinner table.

"You are a real stickler for time," Sofian complained. "Where's Jane?"

"She doesn't work on Wednesdays."

"She is an interesting one." Sofian smiled at the food the maids brought into the dining room. Fadi said nothing. He just took a sip of his drink. Sofian looked at him and frowned a little. "So what has been happening between you and Jane?" he asked.

"Nothing much," Fadi replied. Sofian narrowed his gaze at Fadi.

"Something definitely happened between the two of you." Sofian took a sip of his drink. "You actually cared that she nearly fell over at the refinery, and then you offered her your arm like some kind of gentleman," he continued.

"What is wrong with that?"

"You are not a gentleman and you never offer your hand. In fact, you never want to be seen with a woman's arm linked into yours."

Fadi sighed. Sofian knew him well. They had been friends since they were very young. They had gone to the same schools and now they were in business together. He was the only man Fadi could trust with his life. Obviously, he would be able to tell if something had happened between Jane and Fadi.

"We kissed a few times and now she found out about Faiza. And now she is so upset with me," said Fadi. He wasn't one for details. It was always best to get straight to the point. Sofian burst into laughter. "What is so funny?" Fadi asked.

"You got yourself into a rather messy situation. You did not tell Jane about Faiza?"

"I did not think she needed to know." Fadi picked up a silver fork and started eating.

"Did you apologize to her?"

"Why would I?"

Sofian narrowed his gaze at Fadi. "You are one of the smartest people I know, but you are clueless when it comes to women," he said.

"Women are foreign creatures to me. I know about spending on a woman, I can tell when a woman is attracted to me, I know when she is experienced or inexperienced. However, I never know the right things to say," said Fadi. He shoved a piece of chicken in his mouth. He frowned at how unflavored it was. The new chef's cooking was not as good as Jane's.

"Let me point out your first mistake, you were not honest with Jane from the beginning. Your second mistake was not apologizing to her," said Sofian. He paused to chew on his broccoli, then continued, "She is obviously angry because she has feelings for you and you do not acknowledge them. She probably feels like you were just using her."

"She did tell me to stop playing with her feelings," said Fadi. "She even returned everything that I bought for her."

Sofian raised his eyebrows. "Interesting," he said.

"Why is that interesting?"

"Most women would keep the items, especially if they were expensive items. It shows that she is not a gold digger," he explained. He made a good point. All the women Fadi had ever been with wanted him to spend money on them. Fadi sighed.

"Before she stormed out of my office, she told me to just e-mail her what I wanted her to do," said Fadi. Sofian shook his head.

"She is trying to be casual but that is not going to work. So, what did you do?"

"I e-mailed her work to do."

Sofian started laughing again. "You need to go apologize to her if you care about her and I suspect that you do," he said.

"I don't know about that," Fadi said honestly. He did not know how he felt for Jane. All he knew was that he did not like seeing her upset and he couldn't stop thinking about her. He wanted to make things right. "She slapped me when I kissed her," he said.

Sofian smiled in amusement. "She slapped you? And what did you do about it?" he asked.

"Nothing. I was so shocked, but then again it's Jane. She is so feisty," he said. Sofian burst into laughter.

"You deserved it," he said. Fadi frowned at him. "What about Faiza, is she still here?"

"No, I sent her back to Al Hamri," Fadi replied. The maids filed into the room and started clearing the dinner table. Sofian rubbed his left temple.

"So you have feelings for Jane and not Faiza. You will do yourself and the both of them a disservice if you marry Faiza," he said. Fadi raised his eyebrows.

"What?" he asked.

"If you do not have any feelings for Faiza and you still marry her, she will be miserable. You will be miserable too. Jane will be miserable because the man she loves will have married another woman," he explained. Fadi raised his eyebrows and sighed. He did not want to marry Faiza and was only doing it because of his parents. They really wanted him to marry Faiza. However, he had not thought about breaking the engagement. It was not like he could do it. Faiza was not just an ordinary woman, she was a princess.

"Go speak to Jane. Apologize to her, sincerely," said Sofian.

"Then what?"

"When you talk to her, it will become clear to you if you want to be with her or Faiza. The sooner you choose, the better."

Fadi actually took Sofian's advice. After dinner, he went to Jane's apartment. He stood outside her door for a few minutes before he rang the doorbell. He was not sure what he was going to say, or how Jane was going to react. Was she going to slap him again?

To Fadi's surprise, it was not Jane who opened the door. It was a tall, curvy, dark-skinned woman. She had a beautiful sculpted face and long curly coils of hair. She gasped when she saw him. Her shocked expression quickly turned into an intimidating glare.

"What are you doing here?" she asked him. Fadi raised his eyebrows.

"Do you know me?" he asked her.

"Yes, Fadi. I know who you are."

She had called him by his first name. He wanted to correct her and tell her that it was Sheikh Asaad. However, he was not going to do that. She looked like she would slap him if he said anything wrong. It also seemed that Jane had told her about him. Therefore, he did not want to give Jane more reasons to be angry with him.

"Is Jane home?" he asked.

"Yes she is."

"May I speak to her?"

She folded her arms over her chest and looked at him from head to toe. "It's such a shame that a good-looking man such as yourself doesn't know how to treat women," she said.

"Excuse me?"

"What was Jane to you? A toy? You should have been honest with her from the start. Actually, you should have kept things professional."

She was just as feisty as Jane. "I admit that I did not handle things correctly," he said.

"Who is it?" Fadi recognized Jane's alto voice. How he had missed it.

"It's Fadi," Jane's friend shouted back. Suddenly Jane's head popped out of a room. She stared at Fadi wide-eyed. Fadi resisted the urge to laugh. Jane was adorable as usual. "Shall I let him in?" the friend asked. Jane jerked her head back into the room.

"Let him in, Regina!" she called out. Her friend opened the door wider for Fadi to come in.

"Thank you," he said to her. He went into the room Jane was in. She was standing in the middle of the room with her arms hanging awkwardly at her sides. She wore grey shorts and a white T-shirt. Her hair was tied up messily as usual.

"Are you here for the work that you sent me?" she asked. He had e-mailed her some well-logging data that needed to be interpreted.

"No," Fadi said. For the first time, he felt nervous. He did not know exactly what to say to Jane, and it did not help that her friend was standing in the doorway watching him and listening to him.

"Then what brings you over, Sheikh Asaad?" Jane asked.

"I don't even know where to begin." Apologies were a foreign concept to him. He had gone through life never having to apologize for anything, one of the perks of being a sheikh from a very powerful and wealthy family. He had never had to chase after a woman. They always threw themselves into his arms. However, none of them had been as intriguing, funny, clumsy and feisty as Jane was.

Jane laced her fingers together. "Sir, if there is nothing that you wish to discuss with me, then I shall see you on Friday. I will have the well-logging stuff completed," she said. Her words cut through him like a knife. She spoke to him so formally. It was clear that she was re-establishing a professional boundary between them, and that was not what Fadi wanted.

"You don't have to speak to me so formally," he said to her.

"I should. You are my boss, and I am your employee."

Fadi took a step towards her but she took a step back. "I came here to apologize," he said gently.

Chapter 25

Jane

Jane's jaw hung open in shock. Fadi was standing in the middle of her living room and he was saying that he was there to apologize. She could not believe her ears. He was not the type of man to apologize. The last time they had met, he had acted as though he hadn't done anything wrong.

"Excuse me?" Jane asked him.

"I handled things wrong. I have never been in such a situation," he said to her.

"You definitely handled things horribly."

"I know."

"You are an engaged man. It's not nice being the other woman."

"I told you that I do not love her and that the marriage was arranged by our parents."

"That doesn't make things better," said Jane. Though it did make her feel better that he didn't love Faiza. Part of Jane felt bad for Faiza because it was clear that Faiza had feelings for Fadi.

"It doesn't but that is the reality of the situation. I don't love her, I'm not even sure that I like her," he said. Jane narrowed her gaze and opened her mouth.

"You're not a nice man," said Regina. She was still standing in the doorway eavesdropping on their conversation.

"Tell me about it," Jane agreed.

"I mean that I haven't spent enough time with her to know anything about her. Therefore, I am not sure if I like her because I don't know her," Fadi explained.

"How could you not have spent time with her and yet you are meant to marry her?" Regina asked.

"She is the princess of Al Hamri. Therefore, she couldn't be in the presence of a man. I on the other hand was always working and was never bothered about spending time with her," said Fadi.

"That's weird," said Jane.

"What is?"

"You not wanting to spend time with her."

"Why?"

"She is a beautiful woman."

"Not as beautiful as you are."

Jane's heart flipped in her chest. Fadi had just called her beautiful. It was the first time that he had ever complimented her. She pressed her lips together to stop herself from smiling. She was still upset with him.

"Faiza is not nearly as beautiful or as intelligent and feisty as you are," said Fadi. Oh, he had complimented her again. Jane let out a small laugh.

"I am not that feisty," she said.

"I have never met a woman that speaks her mind like you. Women around me never speak their minds especially to me. No one is brave enough to express their thoughts, especially if they disagree with me. However, you are and it is the first thing I admired about you. That is why I hired you."

Ah! And there it was. The mystery had been solved. Jane had always wondered why he had hired her after she had yelled at him at the end of the interview. So Fadi had liked it. She had not seen that coming at all.

"You liked me speaking carelessly towards you?" she asked. Fadi nodded.

"You were also the first person to ever slap me," he said. Jane smiled.

"You deserved it," she said.

"I did." Fadi took a step towards her. This time she did not move back. "I don't want to marry Faiza. I will fix that situation. Can you be patient with me?"

Before Jane answered, she heard Regina gasp and saw her placing her hand over her chest. Jane shook her head and looked at Fadi. "Patient for what?" she asked. Fadi took her hand into his.

"Don't take either of Roman's offers," he said. He frowned. "I can't even believe that you are on a first-name basis with him."

Jane could not help but burst into laughter. She liked the fact that Fadi was so jealous of Roman. "He's not like other people that insist on being addressed by their titles," she said. She clearly meant Fadi, and he knew that she meant him because he narrowed his gaze at her and tilted his head.

"I ought to stop all my business with that snake," he said. Jane raised her eyebrows.

"Snake?" she questioned.

"He dared to approach my woman behind my back."

Jane and Regina both gasped at the same time. "Your woman?" Jane asked. Was Fadi actually claiming her? She was sure the sky was falling somewhere.

"Yes, Jane Hart. You are my woman and you're going to have to deal with it," he said as he snaked his arm around her waist and kissed her lips. It was so quick, Jane didn't have time to react. "Gosh, I missed these lips," he whispered against her mouth. He released her from his embrace and headed for the door. Jane stood there in shock and watched him leave.

"Regina, what just happened?" Jane whispered after Fadi had left.

"Oh my God, he apologized and claimed you as his woman. Two things that you thought he was never going to do," Regina replied. She approached Jane and took her hands into hers.

"I know, should I believe him?" She desperately wanted to believe him but that was how mistresses were birthed. A man would claim he did not love his wife and the other woman would believe him. Then three years later, the other woman was still by the man's side waiting for him to get divorced.

"I think so. He looked so earnest. I believe him. You could see that it was so hard for him."

Jane smiled. Her insides were melting like butter in a hot pan. Fadi always made her feel like she could fly. It was not easy to let such a man go. "I will give him a chance but with a condition of course," she said.

"What is that?"

"There will be no kissing and touching until he is done with Faiza."

Regina burst into laughter. "Can you handle that?" she asked. It was a good question. Jane was sure that she enjoyed kissing Fadi more than he enjoyed kissing her.

"I will have to," she said before she burst into giggles.

***

Jane was on her way to Fadi's house on Friday night when she received a call from Roman. He invited her to an expensive restaurant for dinner. Jane thought it was the perfect opportunity to straighten things out with him.

"Good evening," Jane greeted the elegant-looking woman behind the booth at the door. "I am here to meet with Roman Waters."

"Please come this way," the woman said with a smile. She led Jane into the dining room. Roman rose to his feet as Jane approached. He wore a black suit and a black shirt. His piercing blue eyes stared at her.

"Miss Hart," he said with a smile as he took her right hand and guided it to his lips. He pressed a gentle kiss against her hand.

"Hello Roman," she said shyly. He pulled out her chair for her. "Thank you," she said as she sat down. Roman sat down opposite her.

"Thank you for coming," he said to her.

"How did you get my number?"

He smiled guiltily. "That kind of information is not difficult to find," he said. It was borderline creepy.

Jane did not know how to feel about it. Jane simply laughed it off.

"You are back sooner than I thought," she said.

"I am just a day early. I couldn't seem to get you off my mind."

Jane raised her eyebrows. "You were thinking about me?" she asked.

"Constantly. It was starting to affect my work. I just couldn't concentrate."

"I find that hard to believe," she said to him. She really did find it hard to believe. There weren't many men that told her that. A waiter approached their table.

"Good evening," he said to them both. "Are you ready to order?"

Jane picked up her menu and quickly looked at it. "You go ahead and order first," she said to Roman.

"I'll have number three please," he said to the waiter.

"I'll have number five please," Jane said to the waiter. It was a steakhouse, so the menu mainly consisted of steak. "I'll have my steak well-done, please."

"Yes ma'am." The waiter jotted down their orders before he disappeared into the kitchen at the back of the restaurant.

Jane and Roman talked as they feasted on their steak. He asked questions about her life. He wanted to know why she wanted to study oil and gas engineering. He also wanted to know about her social life and her family; if she had any siblings and how her childhood was. He was really interested in getting to know to her. It was nice. She wished that Fadi was that interested in getting to know her.

"I will not be taking your offer to work for you," Jane said to Roman after they had finished eating. He wiped his mouth with a napkin and looked at her.

"Why not?" he asked.

"I just started working for Sheikh Asaad. I can't quit now, and I do enjoy my position. I appreciate your kind offer though."

He smiled at her. "I can't say I am not disappointed. I would have loved to work with you," he said.

"Sorry."

"Don't apologize." Roman leaned forward. "May I take you out for dinner again?"

"Um." Jane felt awkward. She had never had to turn someone down. "Maybe but not at the moment," she said.

"Are you seeing someone?"

"It's complicated." It was. Everything with Fadi was complicated.

"I'm not complicated. I am very simple man," he said. Jane laughed. He was simple and straightforward.

"I am just not looking for a new relationship at the moment." Jane frowned a little. She wasn't even in a relationship with Fadi. She did not know what to call it.

"Okay, but I will not give up on you this easily."

Chapter 26

Jane

"You are an hour late," Fadi said to Jane as she walked into the drawing room. He was sitting on the white sofa.

"Hello Fadi. I'm fine, thanks for asking," said Jane.

"Hi." Fadi gestured towards the seat next to him. Jane smiled as she walked over and sat down next to him.

"I had dinner with Roman," she said. Fadi whipped his head in her direction.

"Again?"

"No, this is the first time that we've had dinner. Last time, we had coffee," Jane clarified. Fadi stared at her.

"You shared a meal with him on two occasions." Fadi did not sound pleased at all. It just made Jane want to smile. Fadi getting jealous meant that he cared for her. She reached out and touched his very muscular arm.

"It was just a meal, Fadi, it's not like we are getting married," she said. He narrowed his gaze at her. He was just about to speak when Jane cut him off. "I told him that I don't want to work for him or be in a relationship with him," she said.

"You could have said that to him over the phone." Fadi tried to hide a smile.

"So you know how to smile," said Jane.

"What does that mean?"

"You rarely smile or laugh. It's weird."

Fadi smiled. He leaned closer to Jane. She knew that he was going to kiss her. She quickly threw herself backwards. "No!" she called out as she landed on the sofa backwards.

"What are you doing?" Fadi asked. Jane heaved herself up.

"I wanted to talk to you about this." She cleared her throat. "So, I don't know where we are; if we are in a relationship or not."

"We established that on Wednesday. You are my woman," he said. Jane giggled. It still made her shy; hearing him call her his woman.

"You are still engaged. So until that is sorted out, there will be no kissing."

Fadi raised his eyebrows. "Is that a joke?" he asked.

"I am very serious," she said. She knew it was going to be hard but she was determined.

"And why not?"

"You are engaged and us kissing will really make me feel like I am the other woman."

Fadi smiled as he rubbed his eyebrow. "It won't be easy, but anything for you," he said. Jane leaned closer to him and kissed him on the cheek.

"Thank you," she said.

"That's the first time you've kissed me on the cheek."

"It is." Jane smiled. She felt proud of her boldness. She was confident in many situations but not when it came to men. She had no experience and therefore, she was shy about making the first move.

"I need to go to Al Hamri tomorrow for business. Will you come with me?"

"You want me to come with you?" Jane asked him wide-eyed. Excitement and nerves rushed through her.

"Yes."

"Where will we stay?"

"At my family home, obviously."

Jane's eyes raced. "So I will meet your parents?" she asked.

"Of course," he replied. He took her small hands into his. That was another thing he had never done but Jane was happy about it. She liked the feel of his hands.

"Um, okay. That won't be awkward at all."

Fadi burst into laughter. "It will be fine," he said.

***

Jane arrived at the private airstrip around 11 a.m. Fadi had sent a car to pick her up from her apartment. She was full of mixed emotions. She was excited to go to Al Hamri and see a different country. She wanted to see where Fadi was from and get to know him more. She was excited about working with him and spending more time with him. However, she was nervous about staying in his family home with his family.

The driver parked a few yards away from the jet. He opened the door for Jane and then unloaded her luggage for her. Fadi was waiting for her outside the jet. She got out of the car and rushed over to him.

"Why did you wait outside?" she asked as she approached him.

"I am waiting for you." Fadi kissed her on the forehead.

"It's snowing and it is cold."

"Let's go." Fadi took her hand and led her up the stairs and into the jet. Jane had never flown first class, and now she was flying on a private jet.

They walked into the warm and spacious jet. The interior was cream and dark brown. There were leather chairs with cream and brown cushions. There was a flat-screen television on the wall. Jane wished she could pull out her phone and take pictures to show Regina but that was tacky. She was not going to look like a bumpkin in front of Fadi. Amina was also on the plane. She waved at Jane.

"My brother must really value you," said Amina.

"Why do you say that?" Jane asked as she sat down in the comfortable leather chair opposite Amina.

"You are at his side a lot. You work in his home and now you are coming to Al Hamri with us."

Fadi sat down next to Jane. "Don't mind my sister. She is very nosy," he said.

"I don't think so. She is just being friendly and trying to get to know me," said Jane.

"Yes exactly." Amina smiled at Jane. The flight attendant approached and greeted them all. She asked them to buckle their seatbelts as they were about to take off.

After they had taken off, the flight attendant returned with refreshments. Amina and Jane talked as they ate. Fadi was buried in his tablet. He was always working. It was exhausting for Jane to watch. The man never did anything that was not work related.

"Does your brother know the definition of fun?" Jane asked Amina.

"No." Amina burst into laughter. "He has always been like that, always working. I begged him to take me to the cinema once."

"Did he go with you?"

"Yes but he left after ten minutes."

Jane laughed and shook her head. Fadi looked up from his tablet. "It was a juvenile movie," he defended himself.

"You could have sat through it for the sake of your sister," said Jane. Fadi rolled his eyes and did not bother with a response.

The journey to Al Hamri was very long. In that time, Jane was able to talk to Amina more and just get to know her. She also got a nap. Fortunately for Jane, the seats were very comfortable. It made the long journey bearable. She did not like being confined in the same place for too long. Jane was sitting next to Fadi for the entire flight. She wanted to hold his hand and kiss him but she couldn't. She had made the rule not to kiss him until things were sorted out with Faiza. Jane also did not think Amina knew about their *relationship*.

When the plane landed, Fadi, Jane and Amina unbuckled their seatbelts. They rose from their seats and filed out of the jet. There was a car already waiting for them. The driver loaded their bags into the trunk of the car.

"It's hot," said Jane as she got into the car.

"Of course it is," Fadi replied. He sat in the car next to Jane. Amina sat in the seat opposite them.

"I expected it to be hot but it's just such a sharp change. We were in Boston not too long ago and it was snowing. We are now in blazing hot Al Hamri."

"The two of you are closer than a normal employee and employer," said Amina. She had her eyebrow raised. Jane wanted to just come out and admit that they were in a complicated relationship but that was Fadi's call. It was his sister, and he was the one that was engaged.

"What is it that you want to say?" Fadi asked her.

"You are nicer than you normally are to your employees."

Fadi just narrowed his gaze at her and then looked out of the window. Jane felt a little annoyed with Fadi. That was his moment to tell his sister about their relationship, however he shut it down. Amina did not look convinced. Jane smiled at her and then she looked out of the window.

Al Hamri City was beautiful. Tall palm trees lined the highway. The sky was clear blue. It was such a beautiful environment and Jane looked forward to seeing more of the country. They arrived at the Asaad estate about fifteen minutes later. They drove through huge iron gates and drove up the driveway.

Jane stared out of the window wide-eyed. The estate was massive. She knew that Fadi was from a rich family but she did not expect them to own such a large estate. The car parked outside the house. The house was as big as a hotel. Jane got out of the car and gaped at her surroundings. Miles of green grass stretched away from the house. There were also palm trees around. It looked like a hotel resort.

"Sheikh Asaad," a woman dressed in a white shirt and a black skirt said as she approached them. She had her jet-black hair pinned up. Amina threw her arms around her.

"Hello Maria," he said. Jane raised her eyebrows in shock. Fadi did not greet people. However, he had said hello to Maria. "I trust that you have been well," he added. Amina released Maria from her embrace.

"I have, sheikh," she replied.

"Is mother home?"

"No, she and the sheikh are out of town for a few days. Who is the young lady?" Maria looked at Jane.

"Hello, my name is Jane." Jane extended her hand for her a handshake. Maria shook it firmly.

"She is an engineer and my assistant. I have some business to take care of and I will need her assistance," Fadi said to Maria. She smiled and nodded.

"I will have the main guest room prepared for her." She walked back into the house. The maids followed her with the luggage.

"She is the head maid of the house and a close friend to the family," Fadi said to Jane.

"You'll love her, she is amazing," Amina added.

Jane followed Fadi into the house. The floors were made of black marble. The ceilings were high, and there was a big crystal chandelier. There was an imperial-looking staircase opposite the entrance. Jane followed Fadi up the stairs. There were paintings hung up on the wall.

"I am going to my room," Amina said when they reached the top of the stairs. She touched Jane's arm before she disappeared.

"This way," Fadi said to Jane.

"Your home is beautiful," Jane said to him as they walked down the wide hallways. The maids greeted Fadi as they walked past him. "Where are we going?" Jane asked.

"I am going to show you to your room," Fadi replied.

"Oh?" She was excited to see what it would look like.

"This is where you will stay," Fadi said to Jane when they had arrived.

"Where will you stay?"

"Did you want to share my room?" Fadi had a mischievous look on his face. Jane raised her eyebrows and opened her mouth.

"No," Jane replied.

"I will be staying over there." He pointed at the door at the end of the corridor. It was not that far from hers. "That is my bedroom, if you don't feel like sleeping alone…"

"Goodbye," Jane said before Fadi could finish off his sentence. She turned on her heel and opened the door to the guest room. She heard Fadi laugh behind her as she walked into the room. She smiled to herself and slammed the door shut.

Chapter 27

Jane

The guest room that Jane was staying in was beautifully decorated with marble floors and expensive furniture. The room had a balcony with a view of the green scenery. Jane felt as though she was in a hotel.

"Is the room to your liking?" Maria asked Jane as she walked into the room.

"It's amazing, thank you," Jane replied. "Is Fadi's bedroom really over there?" Jane pointed toward his door. Maria raised her perfectly shaped eyebrows.

"Yes, the sheikh's bedroom is very close by. How long have you worked with the sheikh?"

"Almost four months now."

Maria nodded. "Dinner will be served in about half an hour, if you are hungry," she said. Jane touched her stomach. For the first time, she was not feeling hungry. She was rather feeling tired. It had been such a long journey from Boston.

"If it's okay, I think I will just go to bed," Jane replied.

"Have a good rest." With that, Maria left the room. Jane took her shoes off and threw herself onto the four-poster bed. She was so tired, she fell asleep straightaway.

***

Jane woke up feeling refreshed. She had slept so well. The bed was extremely comfortable and warm. She jumped out of bed and went to have a shower. The guest room had a big, beautiful bathroom. When she finished showering, she went to look for something to wear. Regina had practically packed her suitcase for her because she did not like what Jane liked to wear. Jane preferred tracksuits and shorts; she made no effort to look good. Jane didn't mind Regina helping her out with what to wear.

Jane decided to wear a navy-blue maxi dress. She tied her hair up into a bun. There was a knock on the door. Jane rushed to the door and opened it. There was a maid standing there.

"Good morning, miss," she said.

"Hello," Jane replied with a smile.

"Breakfast will be served in five minutes."

"Okay, I will come down now." Jane rushed back into her room and slipped on some sandals. Then she ran back to the door and followed the maid downstairs.

The dining room was big. There was a white marble-topped table with golden legs and golden chairs in the middle of the dining room. There were cream curtains that matched the table. Amina, Fadi and an unfamiliar young man sat at the table. The man was the first to notice Jane walking into the room. He frowned.

"Who is she?" the man asked. Fadi was reading a newspaper. Jane noticed that he was wearing a white polo shirt. She had always seen him in dress shirts and trousers. Fadi looked up from his paper.

"That's Jane," he replied.

"Morning, Jane," Amina greeted Jane. "Come and sit next to me."

Jane smiled and walked over to the allocated seat. She pulled out the chair for herself and sat down next to Amina.

"Who is Jane though?" the man asked.

"She works with me," Fadi replied. He turned his attention to Jane. "That's my younger brother Beshoy."

"Hello Beshoy. It's good to meet you," Jane said to him.

"You work with my brother?" Beshoy asked.

"Yes, I do."

"And you are joining us for breakfast?"

"He is close to her. It is odd, isn't it?" Amina interjected. Beshoy nodded.

"My brother has never had any employees join us for any meals. Are you staying here, in this house?"

"Yes, I am," Jane replied. Once again Fadi was presented with an opportunity to tell his siblings about his relationship with Jane. She looked at him and waited for his reply.

"Eat your food and leave Jane alone," said Fadi without looking up from his newspaper. Jane narrowed her gaze at him and then looked away. She shrugged her shoulders. She was expecting too much, she told herself. Beshoy and Amina looked at each other. They exchanged questioning glares.

"How long have you worked for my brother?" Beshoy asked Jane.

"Almost four months now," she replied.

"How has it been so far?"

"It's been good," she said. There had been many ups and downs. They had had good times, great times and fights. It was a unique experience. "I am glad to be working at such a reputable company. People at MIT, where I go to school, are dying to work in your family company. I feel blessed," she added. Beshoy nodded.

"What are your plans for the rest of the day?" Amina asked Jane.

"We are going to the rig," Fadi replied. He folded his newspaper and put it down.

"Fadi, it's a Sunday. Can you let Jane just rest for a day? Do you have to work her straight away?"

"I just said we are going to the rig. I wanted to show her around. Besides, we are here for work."

"Why do you care what Jane does? Do you know her?" Beshoy asked Amina.

"Yes, we met in Boston," she replied. Jane just ate her breakfast as she watched the siblings talk about her as if she wasn't there. She studied Beshoy for a moment. He looked much like Fadi. He was just not as muscular or as tall.

"Jane, are you finished eating?" Fadi asked Jane. She took a sip of her juice and nodded. "Okay, let's go," he said as he rose to his feet. Jane quickly sprang up to her feet.

"It was nice meeting you," she said to Beshoy. She turned to Amina and touched her shoulder. "I will see you later," she said to her. Amina smiled at her.

"Don't let my brother give you too much work to do," said Amina. Jane smiled before she followed Fadi out of the room.

They walked out of the house and headed to Fadi's car. The driver was already waiting in the car for them. They both got into the backseat of the car. Jane liked the interior of the car. It was spacious and clean. The seats were made of comfortable soft beige leather.

"You decided to wear a dress today," Fadi said to Jane as they drove off the estate.

"Honestly, I had no idea what to wear. I understand that we are on a work trip, and so I should dress formally. However, it's really hot and we are at your family home," Jane replied.

"Just wear whatever you want." Fadi looked at her. "You look good in that dress. You should wear dresses more often."

Jane laughed a little. "I don't like dresses. It was Regina that packed that dress in my suitcase," she said.

"Your scary friend."

"She isn't scary."

"She was standing in the doorway, ready to beat me up if I said anything wrong to you."

Jane burst into laughter. "Regina and I have been friends for many years. She can be overprotective of me," she said. Fadi smiled. They talked more as they headed to the rig. Jane told Fadi more about her friendship with Regina and their childhood. She also asked Fadi about his siblings. She wanted to know more about his relationships with them and just wanted to know more about him.

When they arrived at the rig, Fadi and Jane met with Sofian. He had flown to Al Hamri a few days before. He greeted Jane with a warm smile. He was always so friendly to her.

"It's your first time to Al Hamri?" he asked Jane.

"Yes, it is," Jane replied.

"It's nice out here. There are beautiful white sand beaches and lots of tourist attractions. Make sure that Fadi shows you around."

Jane burst into laughter. She was definitely interested in visiting all those tourist attractions and the beaches, but she could not picture Fadi walking on the beach with her. She did not think he was interested in such things.

"But why would you suggest my boss show me around?" she asked Sofian. She wondered if he knew about her and Fadi. Why else would he suggest that Fadi show her around? It was a thing for couples or friends.

"He brought you to Al Hamri. Therefore, it is his responsibility to show you around and just make sure that you are comfortable." Sofian flashed a mischievous smile. Jane raised her eyebrows. He definitely knew something. Jane turned to Fadi who maintained a blank expression. He slipped his hands in his pockets and said nothing.

"Shall we look around?" Jane asked. As much as she wanted to hear Fadi's answer about showing her around Al Hamri, she wanted to look around the oil rig.

"Let's go," said Fadi.

The oil rig was quite big. The land stretched for miles. It probably produced a lot of oil. There was large machinery set up, and there were plenty of engineers working. Fadi told Jane that the rig produced a lot of oil. His family owned a lot of land in Al Hamri.

Fadi wanted to refine oil from that rig at his new refinery. As he was telling her his plans, Jane's phone vibrated. She looked at the screen. It was Roman calling her.

Chapter 28

Fadi

"Hey Roman," Jane answered her phone. Fadi raised his eyebrow and looked at her. She was speaking to Roman? Jane walked off to speak to Roman away from Fadi.

"Who is Roman?" Sofian asked Fadi. "As soon as she mentioned his name, your face changed."

"Roman Waters," Fadi spat out.

"Oh, we have business with him. Is that why he is calling her?"

"Probably not. He asked her to work for him." Fadi was feeling annoyed. Why was Roman still calling her?

"So, what did she say?" Sofian asked him.

"She refused."

"So what is the problem?"

"He is interested in her as a woman."

Sofian raised his eyebrows. "That is probably not sitting well with you," he said.

"Obviously not," Fadi replied. He looked at Jane. He couldn't hear what she was saying. He was curious to know what she and Roman were talking about.

"Fadi, are you jealous?" Sofian started laughing. "I never thought I would see this day," he added.

"I do not want that man talking to my woman because I know he has intentions of being with her," said Fadi. Sofian raised his eyebrows.

"Your woman?" he asked.

"Yes, my woman."

"Well, I guess as long as she knows that she is your woman and you treat her right, she has no reason to entertain Roman's feelings for her," said Sofian. Fadi sighed.

"I treat her right," he said.

"Have you ever taken her out for dinner?" Sofian slipped his hands in his pockets. Fadi frowned.

"We had lunch once," he replied.

"Then you need to take her to a nice restaurant for dinner. Make her feel special. Have you claimed her as your woman?"

"Of course I have."

"I mean, have you introduced her as your woman? Since she will be staying in your home, did you tell your family that she was your woman?"

"No." Fadi frowned. "I told them she is my assistant."

"Oh gosh." Sofian shook his head. "I don't think she liked that."

"Well, she is my assistant. She works for me."

Sofian hung his head and shook it. "You should have introduced her as your woman. She was probably hurt by you introducing her as your assistant. She probably thought that you were embarrassed by her or that you don't care for her," he said. Fadi sighed. It had not occurred to him. He had never had to introduce anyone as his woman. He had never introduced any woman that he was in a relationship with to his family.

"You are right," he said. Jane finished up on the phone and walked back to him.

"What did he want?" Fadi asked Jane.

"Roman? He called just to find out how I was and if I had changed my mind about meeting him for dinner," Jane replied. Fadi and Sofian looked at each other.

"He is persistent."

"It will be awkward working with him now," said Sofian. "Maybe we shouldn't work with him."

"That is ridiculous," said Jane. "I am not going to date him. You shouldn't stop working with him because you feel jealous or something." Jane whipped her head in Sofian's direction with her eyes widened. Sofian smiled.

"I already knew about your relationship with Fadi," he said and then grinned at her.

"Oh," Jane said quietly.

"I don't like him calling you," Fadi said to Jane. She nodded.

"I understand but I told him that I am not interested in him. Besides it's not me that is calling him," she said to him. Fadi pressed his palm against her neck and his thumb on her cheek and pulled her closer. He kissed her forehead.

"Okay," he said. "Let's go."

"Sofian, it was good to see you again," Jane said.

"Likewise," Sofian replied with a smile. Jane and Fadi headed back to the car.

"Where are we going now?" Jane asked Fadi as they got into the car. He looked at his watch. It was almost midday.

"Let's go for lunch," he said. He asked the driver to take them to one of his favourite restaurants in Al Hamri.

"I forget that you are Arabic," Jane said to Fadi.

"Why?"

"Just because when I am around you, we speak in English. When I hear you speak in Arabic, it sounds nice."

"Would you like to learn how to speak it?"

Jane raised her eyebrows. "I've never been good at learning languages. My tongue is stubborn. It doesn't get the pronunciations right," she said.

"Maybe you had the wrong teacher," Fadi said with a smile. Jane smiled back at him.

"Okay, teach me. The easy words first."

"Repeat after me, *habibi*."

"Habibi," she said. Her pronunciation was not good but she sounded adorable. "What does that mean?" she asked. Fadi grinned at her.

"It's how you should address me. It means beloved," he replied. Jane burst into laughter.

"Oh really?" she asked and started laughing again.

"Yes." Fadi leaned closer to her. Just when his face was inches closer to hers, she turned to the side.

"I told you, we are not kissing until you have dealt with your situation," she said. Her cheeks turned bright red. Fadi caressed her cheek with the back of his hand.

"I miss kissing you," he said and kissed her cheek. Jane let out a giggle.

"Then you better do something about it."

Fadi laughed as he sat up straight. She was right. It was not fair to her for him to be caught in between two women. The car came to a halt. They had arrived at the restaurant.

"We are here." Fadi opened his door. Jane opened hers too and got out of the car. Fadi led her to the restaurant. As soon as they walked in, the guests gasped. They stared at him, and some of them tried to greet Fadi. A waiter immediately approached them and ushered them to the private area where Fadi dined whenever he was in town.

"This is a nice place," Jane said to Fadi as they sat down in the black leather chairs. The waiter placed the menus on the table and drew the red curtains before he left.

"It is," he replied. They both picked up their menus.

"You can order for me. I am sure you know what is best here." Jane smiled.

"Okay." Fadi called for the waiter and ordered some food for them.

Lunch was an interesting affair. Fadi had taken Jane to the restaurant per Sofian's advice. He wanted to take her out for dates and get to know her more than he already did. He wanted to make their bond stronger. Jane was very open with him. She shared a lot with him and it was nice.

After lunch Fadi and Jane returned to Fadi's family home. When they walked into the house, they found Fadi's parents standing by the stairs. His mother's face lit up as soon as she saw her son. She approached him and kissed him on both cheeks.

"This is a pleasant surprise," she said.

"I came on Saturday but you weren't here. You and father had a nice trip?" Fadi said to his mother.

"Yes, we did," his father replied as he approached also. Amina came rushing down the stairs. No doubt she had heard that their parents were back. She approached them and wrapped her arms around her father.

"I missed you so much," she said to their parents. Her father kissed her on the forehead.

"Who is this young lady?" Fadi's father asked Fadi and then looked at Jane. She was standing at his side awkwardly and playing with her fingers.

"This is my woman," said Fadi.

Chapter 29

Jane

"She is what?" Fadi's mother said calmly. Amina gasped and covered her mouth with her hand. Beshoy was just walking down the stairs. His eyes widened as he rushed towards them. Jane was just as shocked as they all were. Fadi had been asked a couple of times who she was and he had introduced her as his employee.

"Her name is Jane and she is my woman," Fadi repeated. His father raised his eyebrows and then looked at Jane. Beshoy and Amina stared at Jane with faces full of curiosity. Jane didn't know what to say. She had so badly wanted Fadi to publicly claim her as his woman but she had not anticipated the awkwardness. She wished that he had introduced her as his woman to one person at a time, not in front of everyone like this. It was incredibly awkward.

"Correct me if I am wrong, but your woman is Faiza. That is whom you are engaged to," said his mother. Fadi's mother wore a nice white dress and pearls. She looked beautiful and elegant. Jane was curious as to how his mother was going to feel about her.

"We were betrothed at a young age, but she was never my woman," said Fadi.

"Son, I am confused," said his father.

"I wanted to speak to you all and let you know that I want to break the engagement between myself and Faiza."

"Oh my God." Fadi's mother placed her hand on her heart.

"This is interesting." His father looked at Jane and studied her for a moment. "Are you sleeping with my son?"

"No sir," Jane replied.

"Did you know that he was betrothed to another?"

"I found out just last week."

Gasps filled the air. Jane knew that she probably shouldn't have said that but there was nothing that she could have said that wouldn't have shocked anyone. She could have just simply said yes I knew, but that would make her look like an opportunist and a mistress. If she had said no, then they would all wonder why she was not reacting to the news. It would also make Fadi look bad in front of his family. She decided that the truth was the best in that situation.

"There is no way you are breaking the engagement with Faiza," said his mother. She turned to face Jane. "Did you purposely seduce my son because of who he is?" she asked.

"No ma'am," Jane replied. She knew nothing about seduction. There is no way that she would have been able to seduce Fadi or any man and make him leave his betrothed. She did not have that skill.

"I can't accept this. The wedding is next month," said his mother. Jane's eyes widened. She had no idea that the wedding was so close.

"It is best that I break the engagement off. I have never wanted Faiza to be my wife. I only agreed just to please you and father," said Fadi. His father rubbed his temples.

"We need to talk about this," he said. "Let's go to the drawing room."

"I don't even want her in my house," said Fadi's mother.

"Can you excuse us?" Fadi's father said to Jane. He looked at Amina and Beshoy. "The two of you should leave also."

"Please go back to America and just leave my son alone," his mother said to Jane.

"Please don't speak to her like that," Fadi said to his mother. He placed his hand on her lower back. "Go upstairs and wait for me," he said to her so gently. Jane nodded and rushed upstairs. She went to wait in her room. Moments later, there was a knock on her door. She opened it and found Amina and Beshoy standing there.

"Hi," Jane said awkwardly.

"I can't believe you and Fadi left me in the dark," Amina said as she walked into the room. Beshoy followed her in. Jane shut the door after them.

"Our relationship is very complicated. It was not up to me to tell you. That was his place," Jane said to Amina. Fadi's siblings sat down on the sofa in Jane's room.

"Are you and my brother getting married?" Beshoy asked. Jane gasped and widened her eyes.

"No," she said with red cheeks. The thought of marrying Fadi had not crossed her mind. However, after hearing the question from Beshoy, she was now entertaining the idea. She knew that four months was not long enough but she had never been with any man for that long. She was in love and there was no denying it. However, Fadi's mother was not ready to allow their relationship. It worried and upset Jane.

"He is about to break his engagement to the princess of the country just to be in a relationship with you?" Beshoy asked.

"I didn't know about Faiza from the beginning. I did not target Fadi just because he is a sheikh. I just met him when I applied for a job as his housekeeper. I only found about Faiza when she came to visit him," she said. Amina shook her head.

"He was wrong to keep you in the dark like that," she said.

"He was wrong to keep us in the dark like that," said Beshoy.

For the next hour, Beshoy and Amina asked Jane all the questions they could come up with. They asked how things started between herself and Fadi. They also asked questions about Jane; her life, family, education, aspirations, relationships and traits. It felt as though Jane was at a police station getting interrogated.

***

Fadi

Fadi had been arguing with his parents for the past hour but they were still not in agreement. He did not want to marry Faiza but his mother wasn't hearing it. She really wanted him to marry Faiza.

"This is an important marriage. You can't just ruin it because your hormones went wild," said Fadi's mother.

"It's not about my hormones. I never wanted to marry Faiza. I am sure you noticed that I was never enthusiastic about the entire thing," Fadi replied.

"Son, I know that you weren't happy about the idea of getting married. However, this marriage was

236

arranged many years ago. We can't just break it now," said Fadi's father. He was calmer than his wife.

"Faiza and I would not be happy in this marriage."

"So, you want us to go to the palace and tell the king that you do not want to marry his only daughter?" said Fadi's mother.

"I will tell him myself," Fadi replied. His mother looked at him as though he had lost his mind.

"And then you want to marry that woman? She's not even Arabic." His mother shook her head. It was bad enough that Fadi did not want to marry Faiza, it was even worse that he wanted to be with a Western woman. His mother was not going to agree to it easily.

"I finally met a woman that I can be comfortable with, a woman that shares the same passion for the oil and gas industry. Jane is smart, beautiful and funny. She doesn't care about my money. Instead of being happy for me, you want to stop me from being with someone that would make me happy," he said to his mother.

"You never gave Faiza a chance. She could have been the woman for you," said his mother.

"She wouldn't have been," he replied.

"I am so disappointed in you." His mother rose to her feet and left the room in tears. He never wanted his mother to cry but he didn't see why she was crying over him choosing happiness. People always said that Fadi was a cold and uncaring man. Now that he was showing a more sensitive side for someone that he had fallen in love with, his parents couldn't accept Jane. They couldn't even be happy for him.

"I have done nothing for her to be disappointed in me. I just fell in love. Is that such a bad thing?" Fadi said to his father. The older sheikh was silent for a moment.

"I don't agree with how you went about things. You should have refused to be betrothed with Faiza from the beginning," he said. Fadi raised his eyebrows.

"It wasn't so easy saying no to the king and to you and mother. You were all so invested in this marriage. I thought it would be okay. I never expected to find love elsewhere."

"I know, son." His father nodded. "I also know that love is hard to find."

"Jane is special and I can't let her go."

"You have to tell the king yourself and you have to deal with the fallout."

Fadi nodded. He was prepared to do anything for Jane. He wasn't too surprised at how well his father was taking the situation. His father was always so laid-back and he was very much like Fadi. His father was quicker to understand Fadi's needs. His mother was more driven by emotions and didn't always understand Fadi.

After his talk with his father, Fadi went upstairs to check on Jane. He found her in her room with Amina and Beshoy. He already knew that his siblings were asking her so many questions.

"Can the two of you give Jane and me some privacy?" Fadi said as he walked into Jane's bedroom.

"What did mother say?" Amina asked.

"Just go."

Amina frowned at Fadi before she and Beshoy left the room. Fadi sat down on the sofa next to Jane. He took her hands into his and kissed them.

"Are you okay?" she asked him.

"I love you," he said to her. The words just came out so easily. He had never said them to anyone. Jane stared at him wide-eyed. She didn't say anything for a moment.

"You can say something, you know," he said to her.

"I'm sorry." Jane laughed. "No one has ever said that to me."

"I always knew that you had never been with anyone else."

Jane rolled her eyes and smiled. "And I don't want to be with anyone else. I love you too," she said. Fadi pulled her into his arms and kissed her so gently and slowly.

Chapter 30

Fadi

"Repeat yourself," the king said to Fadi. The king was sitting in his red and gold chair staring at Fadi with his eyebrows crossed. On the Monday morning, Fadi had gone to the palace and asked to see the king.

"I do not think that I am the right man for your daughter," said Fadi.

"So what are you saying to me?"

"I would like to break off the engagement."

The king raised his grey eyebrows. He was a short-tempered man. Fadi was worried about how he was going to respond. The king was also very overprotective of his only daughter.

"You do not want to marry Faiza?" the king asked.

"Yes, your majesty," Fadi replied. The king rubbed his temples.

"I can't believe what I am hearing. You want to break this engagement off because you do not feel that you are the right man for Faiza?"

"That is correct. Faiza and I have nothing in common. We have never been able to build a bond or relationship. I don't think marriage will be right for us."

"The wedding was scheduled for next month."

"I regret that I did not do this sooner."

"This is outrageous. I can't allow this. You will marry my daughter."

"If we still got married, neither Faiza nor I would be happy in that marriage," he said. Suddenly Faiza and her mother walked into the room. Fadi took a deep breath. Things were about to get more complicated.

"I hear that Sheikh Asaad was here," Faiza said as she entered the drawing room. She and her mother sat in the chairs with the king and Fadi.

"I would rather the two of you did not participate in this conversation," the king said to Faiza and his wife.

"Why not?" the queen asked. The king rubbed his temples again.

Fadi looked at Faiza. "You are a beautiful woman," he said to her.

"Thank you."

"I believe that you will find someone better than me."

"What are you saying?"

"We should not get married." Fadi felt it was better to just get straight to the point. Faiza and her mother both gasped. The king shook his head.

"What?" Faiza's face turned red. "The wedding is next month."

The queen shook her head quietly. She looked more hurt than angry.

"Why? I thought we got along fine," said Faiza.

"We get along but we have nothing in common. We are too different and we don't love each other. I don't think this marriage would be good for either one of us," said Fadi. Faiza sprang to her feet.

"I am the princess of Al Hamri. I will not have you embarrass me like that. I am too good for you. I will find someone else." Faiza rushed out of the room in tears.

"I had a feeling that you did not like my daughter," said the queen. "You never called her or came to visit her. At first I thought you were just being respectful but then it dawned on me that you don't have feelings for her."

"I am sorry. I never wanted to hurt or disappoint you," Fadi said to the queen. She quietly rose to her feet.

"It's best to call off the engagement now, rather than right before the wedding or to have a divorce." With that said, she left the room.

"I do not want to see you or your family ever again. We will not invest in any of your businesses," the king said to Fadi. He was being petty but Fadi understood that he was hurt and annoyed by Fadi calling off the engagement.

"I understand," Fadi replied.

"Get out of my sight."

Fadi rose to his feet. He bowed his head to the king before he walked out of the room. He sighed with relief as he walked out. He was glad that the engagement was broken. Obviously, there were a lot of people angry at him, but he had to do it.

When Fadi arrived back home, he found his mother dragging a suitcase out of the house and dumping it on the ground. She walked back into the house. Fadi got out of the car and rushed into the house. He wanted to see what was going on.

"Get out of my house and never come back," Fadi's mother shouted. Fadi saw his mother escorting Jane down the stairs.

"What is happening here?" Fadi asked.

"I don't want to see her."

Fadi frowned. "Please don't treat her like that," Fadi said to his mother.

"She is a jezebel. It's because of her that your engagement with Faiza has been broken off," his mother replied. She was so angry, Fadi was worried that she was going to slap Jane or something. Fadi quickly approached them and took Jane's arm. He pulled her closer to him and pushed her behind his back.

"Jane is not like that at all. I broke off the engagement with Faiza because yes, I love Jane, and I have never wanted to get married to Faiza. Please be understanding," he said.

"I want her out, right now!" she screamed. There was no reasoning with her. His father walked down the stairs.

"The king just called and he did not have a lot of nice things to say," said Fadi's father. Fadi raised his eyebrows.

"The king himself called?" he asked.

"Yes. So you can imagine how angry he was."

Fadi shrugged his shoulders. "It had to be done," he said. He knew that the king wasn't going to take it well but he still had to do it.

"It had to be done?" his mother spat out.

"Please calm down."

"Don't tell me to calm down." His mother looked at Jane. "Just get out, right now." She took off her pearl necklace and threw it at Jane. "If it's money that you want, then take that necklace and sell it," she called out. Jane just turned on her heel and walked out.

"I can't believe you just did that," Fadi said to his mother. "Now I am disappointed in you." He turned on his heel and followed Jane out. She was about to pick up her suitcase when he took her hand and pulled her towards his car.

"Wait!" she called out.

"Leave it," he said. He opened the passenger door for her. "Get out," he told the driver. The driver quickly got out of the car. Fadi got into the driver's side and drove off the estate. He took her to the airport. He was so angry at his mother; he was going to return to Boston with Jane.

When they arrived at the airport, they both got out of the car and headed into the jet. They sat down as they waited for it to get fueled up.

"I don't think you should leave things like that with your family," Jane said to Fadi. She leaned closer to him and took his hands into hers.

"Leave things like what? My mother disrespected you and I was not going to allow her to continue being rude to you."

"I appreciate that but she is still your mother."

Fadi turned his head to face her. "They should be happy for me that I found the woman I love," he said to her. Jane reached out and touched his face.

"It's hard for them right now. They were prepared for your wedding with Faiza but then just a month before, you told them that you did not want to marry her. They need to process this," she said to him. She leaned forward and pressed her lips against his. Fadi looked into her eyes and realized how lucky he was. Even though his parents were not accepting her, she was not saying anything bad about them. She was telling him to be more understanding and give them time.

***

Jane

"Finally!" Jane shouted as she walked into her apartment. She took her coat off and hung it up. She shook the snow off her leather boots. "It's finally Christmas break!" she cried out. She was excited to have a couple weeks away from lectures and assignments. It had been a month since she had been in Al Hamri. Things had been going great between herself and Fadi. However, his mother still didn't acknowledge their relationship.

Jane frowned as she walked towards the living room. There were white and red rose petals on the floor.

What was Jason up to? she asked herself. He always did such romantic things for Regina.

"What the hell?" Jane spat out when she walked into the living room. She found her parents in there with Regina, Jason, Fadi, Sofian, Amina and Beshoy. The room was filled with rose petals and candles. The lights were dimmed. Everyone was looking at her with goofy grins on their faces.

"What is going on?" Jane asked. Fadi approached her. He was wearing a black tuxedo. He looked as handsome as always. He walked towards Jane and stopped right in front of her.

"I never understood the meaning of love until I met you. I never thought I would love anyone or that I would even be capable of loving anyone," he said to her.

"Um, okay." Jane felt extremely awkward and shy. Fadi dropped to one knee. Jane's eyes flew wide open. "What are you doing?" she whispered.

"I love you and I need you in my life," he said. He was being all romantic and sweet. It was unlike him. "Be my wife," he said.

"Huh?" Jane was not sure that she had heard correctly. Fadi fished a little red velvet box out of his pocket and flipped it open. Jane's eyes widened when she saw the ring inside. It had a huge diamond in the middle.

"Marry me," he said.

"I… I…" Jane could not even get the words out. She felt like she was going to pass out from the shock. Fadi was the man of her dreams but she never thought that she was the woman for him.

"Say yes!" Regina and Jane's mother cried out in unison.

"Yes," Jane said. Fadi smiled and slipped the ring on her finger. He rose to his feet and kissed her. Everyone cheered and clapped.

"Congratulations!" Amina cried out as she ran into Jane's arms. She held her so tightly. Everyone approached and took their turns hugging and congratulating Jane and Fadi.

"How did you get everyone here?" Jane asked Fadi.

"Fadi and Regina came to visit us two weeks ago. He spent the last two weeks convincing us that he was the man for you. He asked us for your hand in marriage," said Jane's mother. Jane raised her eyebrows and looked at him.

"I wanted everything to be a surprise," he said.

"I helped to pick out the ring," Regina said with a big smile on her face. Jane smiled and hugged Fadi. She was perfectly happy. She had found the man of her dreams. She was worried that his parents did not accept their relationship but at least his siblings and her parents did.

"I love you," he whispered in her ear.

"I love you too," she replied.

Epilogue

"Hello Maria," Jane said with a nervous smile on her face.

"Hello Jane," she replied. Her eyes searched the vicinity.

"Fadi isn't here. I came alone. I would like to see Lady Asaad." Jane couldn't go through with the wedding knowing that his mother wouldn't be there. She had to try and speak to her.

"Come in." Maria led Jane to the drawing room, where Fadi's parents were. Maria cleared her throat before she spoke. "Excuse me, Sheikh Asaad and Lady Asaad," she said. The couple turned their heads and looked at the door. Fadi's mother gasped.

"What is she doing here?" she said.

"I came to see you," said Jane. Fadi's mother laughed sarcastically.

"I heard that you succeeded in getting my son to marry you. Are you here to rub it in my face?"

"Let her speak first," said Fadi's father. Jane knew that Fadi's father wasn't so against her relationship with Fadi. He had tried to convince his wife to give in but she was too stubborn. Jane boldly walked into the room and sat down at the sofas with them. Maria raised her eyebrows.

"I love Fadi as a man not as a sheikh. I don't care about money and power," she said.

"How am I supposed to believe that?" his mother asked. It had already been four month since they got engaged. Their wedding was only weeks away. She had hoped by that time Fadi's mother would have gotten over her anger but apparently she hadn't.

"I have a prenuptial agreement." Jane fished out the document from her purse and placed it on the table. "I had Fadi's lawyer draw up an agreement to say that if we ever got divorced, I would get nothing," she said. Fadi's father raised his eyebrows.

"You did that?" he asked. "You know that my son is worth billions?"

Jane nodded. "I am aware but like I said, it's not about the money for me. I truly love him," she said.

"Will you claim an allowance from him during the marriage?" his mother asked.

"Absolutely not. I will work and get my own salary. He will be my husband and not my bank," she said. Fadi's parents looked at the document. They were both speechless.

"The younger sheikh does seem happy with her," Maria said quietly. Everyone turned their heads to face her. "I am just saying."

"He is happy. I just hope that you would be happy for him," Jane said to his parents. She rose to her feet and left the room.

***

The rehearsal dinner was being held at Fadi's house. Everyone sat the table eating and laughing. Jane's family and friends had attended. Fadi's siblings, his father and a few friends had attended. Even Mariam was there. She had finally let her feelings for Fadi die. She was a bit shocked when she heard about Fadi marrying Jane but she supported whatever Fadi did. Suddenly Maria and Fadi's mother walked into the dining room.

"Oh my God!" Jane cried out.

"Mother?" Fadi said.

"I couldn't miss my eldest son's wedding," she said. Fadi and Jane both rose to their feet. Jane smiled and placed her hands on her heart.

"You mean that?" he asked.

"I came here, didn't I?" She approached Fadi and Jane. She hugged her son tightly.

Then she kissed Jane on both cheeks before she hugged her.

"At last!" Amina cried out.

"I'm sorry for how I treated you. I can only make it better by being a good mother-in-law to you," Fadi's mother said to Jane.

"Thank you. I appreciate that," Jane said to her. Everyone clapped and cheered. Fadi smiled and kissed his mother on both cheeks. Everything was finally in place. Jane and Fadi could now get married in peace. Everyone that mattered was going to attend their wedding. Business was going great. Fadi's refinery was bringing in profits and he was on track to make all his money back that he had invested. Roman had given up on Jane after she told him about her engagement to Fadi. He was jealous of Fadi but he knew that he had to give her up. There was no chance for him after she found the man of her dreams.

What to read next?

If you liked this book, you will also like *In Love with a Haunted House*. Another interesting book is *The Oil Prince*.

In Love With a Haunted House

The last thing Mallory Clark wants to do is move back home. She has no choice, though, since the company she worked for in Chicago has just downsized her, and everybody else. To make matters worse her fiancé has broken their engagement, and her heart, leaving her hurting and scarred. When her mother tells her that the house she always coveted as a child, the once-famed Gray Oaks Manor, is not only on the market but selling for a song, it seems to Mallory that the best thing she could possibly do would be to put Chicago, and everything and everyone in it, behind her. Arriving back home she runs into gorgeous and mysterious Blake Hunter. Blake is new to town and like her he is interested in buying the crumbling old Victorian on the edge of the historic downtown center, although his reasons are his own. Blake is instantly intrigued by the flame-haired beauty with the fiery temper and the vulnerable expression in her eyes. He can feel the attraction between them and knows it is mutual, but he also knows that the last thing on earth he needs is to get involved with a woman determined to take away a house he has to have.

The Oil Prince

A car drives over a puddle and muddy water splashes Emily, who was just out for a walk, from head to toe. When she sees the car parked at a gas station moments later, she decides to confront the man leaning against it. The handsome man refuses to apologize, and after hearing what Emily thinks about him, watches her leave. The next day, fate plays a joke on Emily when she finds out that the man is her boss's brother and a prince of a Middle Eastern country. Prince Basil often appears in tabloids because of different scandals and in order to tame his temper, his father sends him to work on a project of drilling a methane well in Dallas. If Basil refuses or is unsuccessful, his financial accounts will be blocked and his title of prince will be revoked. Although their characters clash, Emily and Basil fall in love while working together and Basil's heart melts. When the project that can significantly improve his family business hits a major obstacle, Basil proves that love has tremendous power and shows a side of himself that nobody knew existed.

About Kate Goldman

In childhood I observed a huge love between my mother and father and promised myself that one day I would meet a man whom I would fall in love with head over heels. At the age of 16, I wrote my first romance story that was published in a student magazine and was read by my entire neighborhood. I enjoy writing romance stories that readers can turn into captivating imaginary movies where characters fall in love, overcome difficult obstacles, and participate in best adventures of their lives. Most of the time you can find me reading a great fiction book in a cozy armchair, writing a romance story in a hammock near the ocean, or traveling around the world with my beloved husband.

One Last Thing...

If you believe that *Maid For a Sheikh* is worth sharing, would you spend a minute to let your friends know about it?

If this book lets them have a great time, they will be enormously grateful to you – as will I.

Kate

www.KateGoldmanBooks.com

Manufactured by Amazon.ca
Bolton, ON